A Complex Journey

Book Two

The Next Day

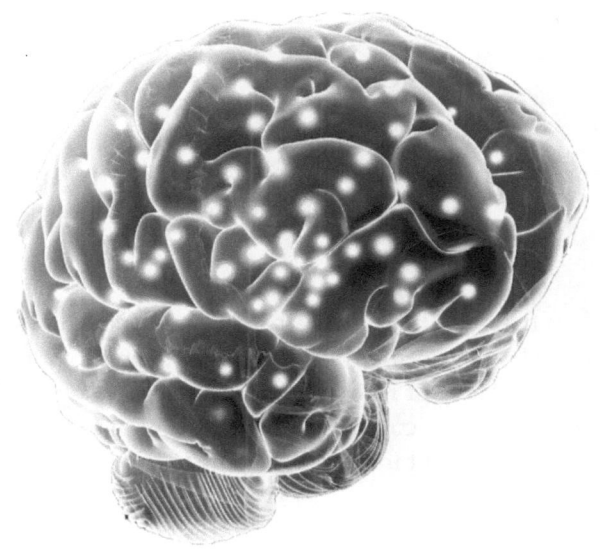

Randy McIntosh

Mouse Gate Press.
1103 Middlecreek
Friendswood, Texas 77546
281-992-3131 TEX
www.totalrecallpress.com

Copyright © 2022 by Randy McIntosh
Book Cover Graphics By Jessica Palmer
All rights reserved

ISBN: 978-1-64883-134-8
UPC: 6-43977-41348-2

FIRST EDITION
1   2   3   4   5   6   7   8   9   10

This is for the folk who go to great efforts to make complicated things understandable.

About the Author

Randy McIntosh is an aspiring fiction writer and established neuroscientist studying brain health and aging for over 25 years. He has an extensive scientific publication record on topics ranging from learning and memory functions in the brain to analytics and computer modeling of brain networks. He has built an open-source brain modeling platform, *TheVirtualBrain* (http://thevirtualbrain.org), in with his two close collaborators in Europe. His first short story, "For the Cost of Steak Dinner" about an interview with a retired hitman appeared in Adelaide Literary Magazine.

Randy is also an amateur musician, enjoying weekend gigs at local cafés in Vancouver, where he and his wife reside.

Preface

I am a scientist who has studied brain networks and complexity for almost thirty years. I want to provide the public with knowledge to better understand the seeming randomness in our world. Climate, economy, genetics, and immunology are complex systems that are inherently hard to predict. If we had a better intuition about complex systems, things like climate change and the recent pandemic might be better appreciated. The subtext of the book is teaching basic ideas about complex systems, but wrap this in fun Sci-Fi narrative.

Introduction

In Book One we met three scientists (Katya, Logan and Terry—aka the trio) who have developed a brain simulation platform based on principles of Complex Adaptive Systems, called "BrainMaze". The trio have made significant advances in medicine by developing the platform that can use a person's own brain to create an avatar lives within the BrainMaze platform. Simulations done in BrainMaze test potential treatments first in the avatar before going to the patient. The success in the medicine leads to an even greater success for BrainMaze as a tool for people to interact through a Brain-Computer Interface.

This occurs when the world is on the brink of a crisis. Political upheaval from the declining influence of the USA and UK results in the establishment of a more distributed governing structure, similar to the European Union, called the Global Council. The Council installs a worldwide AI system that enables sharing of resources globally to remedy food shortages and economic imbalance.

Climate change, however, continues to cause significant problems. Flooding disrupts much of the infrastructure in coastal cities, and extreme heat and cold destroy much of the capacity to maintain healthy infrastructure. The Global Council approaches the trio to see if their BrainMaze system can help. The trio proposes to set up an interface between the Council's AI system and BrainMaze to combine the best of both systems (i.e., the whole is greater than the sum of its parts). Two key members of the council, the Chair Sara Meyer, Secretary Sebastian Baren, are the major advocates for the trio's plan.

After the council meeting, Sebastian informs the trio of the ulterior motive for their recruitment. There is suspicion among the council that someone has hacked into the Global AI system, but their attempts to identify the source have been unsuccessful. Sebastian asks the trio to work directly with a special ops team to further investigate the Global AI problem. TechStaff, an engineering wizard who works for the council, sets up a bootcamp for the trio where they meet the rest of the special ops group at HQ, which is led by the Chair, Sara Meyer. Each member of the trio is assigned a bodyguard, who received codenames to help hide their identities: "BG" followed by the initial of the trio member they are assigned to (e.g., BGL is bodyguard for Logan, BGK for Katya, and BGT for Terry). Yvette, a former student with Logan, is also a member of this special ops team.

The trio uses BrainMaze to analyze the communications patterns of the Global AI, identifying a potential weak spot in Malaysia. The team travels to Councillor Xi's compound near Kuala Lumpur to examine the local AI system more closely. Xi's team tells them of a mysterious green ooze that is affecting the water supply. The team travels to a makeshift temple that has a high concentration of the green ooze. Inside the temple, the team finds a large pool of the green ooze but while investigating, black and white humanoids emerge from the pool. The humanoids are unaffected by the team's weapons. While trying to escape, temple goers who accuse them of violating the temple's sanctity confront the team. A battle follows and Terry's bodyguard, BGT, is seriously injured.

Table of Contents

Chapter One:
A long slumber

Terry in Prison

Green

Terry's eyes snapped open. He wasn't sure if he heard the word in his head or if it was spoken to him.

GREEN

He realized he was lying down in a sort of fetal position. Why, where, how, and when was not clear.

At the edge of his sight, he could make out a green wall. As he pushed himself upright, he felt like he'd been in a long slumber. Still a bit groggy, but rested. His back and arms were tight. He sat and examined the room.

He remembered watching as two vehicles boxed their own vehicle off the road. After their car had stopped, he was grabbed from the passenger seat and struggled before losing consciousness. *How did it move so fast?* he wondered. *How did it get inside without breaking a window?*

The walls were an odd hue. It seemed to be organic and artificial at the same time. He scanned above and saw the same green in the ceiling. Featureless, save for the perceptible intersections of the walls and ceiling, it was an odd choice of colour for a room, one he had seen before. The floor bothered him. It was black, but not black. The section where the wall and floor met looked like the wall disappeared. The black did not reflect.

It did not have the dull sheen like a matte paint but looked like, well, nothing.

He felt a slight tinge of panic as he thought, maybe there is no floor, but his body's position suggested something could hold his weight. He moved his hand across the floor, *So, this is what black feels like.*

"Are you okay, Professor?" he heard. He wasn't sure if it was spoken to him or was in his head. Terry stood upright. The impression of standing on nothing was unsettling.

"We're sorry to take you away from your team," came the next phrase.

"I am assuming I am talking to the Aliens," Terry said aloud. His voice trailed off abruptly; there was no echo in the room. He started walking forward slowly, expecting the floor to give way at any moment.

"Is that what you call us? Okay, if that makes you comfortable, we can go with that."

As his vision got used to the room's odd light, the green changed slightly its hue in sections. The change travelled from one section to another, then moved in another direction.

As his head cleared, he realized that this green was indeed the same green he had seen before; it was a liquid mass. This meant the walls might be some sort of glass, and he was surrounding the green liquid. The light must come from it, but the absolute black of the floor consumed it, leaving an uncomfortable feeling of being suspended over a black abyss.

"Do you guys market your decorating skills? I know people who would love a floor like this."

"We can discuss that later, Professor. First, we need you to understand what we are doing here."

"I think I have a pretty good idea." He touched one wall and withdrew his hand when his palm sunk into the green.

"We know our doing this without the Global Council knowledge is unsettling," the Alien commented.

"To say the least, yes." Terry continued to scan the ceiling and walls. The green was not behind a glass wall. It was the wall.

The Alien continued, "But you need to know that despite the advances your society has made, you still do not understand all the implications of how the AI system you designed works."

Terry realized that the voice he perceived was neither spoken nor in his head. It was like he was imagining text, but the text spoke to him. This also meant there was no real voice as the words changed between female, male, child or adult in mid-phrase.

He took a deep breath. "Look, from what we've been able to find out, you are about to trigger a cataclysmic event that will wipe out much of the Pacific coastal communities. You'd think that the people who live there would want a little warning, and that's what we were going to do before you stopped us. Don't you think they deserve that?" he said. His words came out more aggressively than he would have liked.

"We appreciate your passion, Professor. But you have not learned the system as well as you might believe."

"Well, we did design it. I think we understand a lot."

"You built a tool based on Complex Adaptive Systems, but you do not understand the theory."

"Yeah, yeah, don't use a tool unless you understand the principle."

"Exactly. Take a moment and consider what brought you here. We're sure that you will have a better appreciation for what we are trying to do."

The hue changes in the green stopped and became uniform.

"Is this because we captured one of your team in the sewer? Are you mad about that?" There was no response as the black absorbed Terry's words. "Hmm, I guess we're done talking."

The hue changes in the green stopped and became uniform.

Terry sat down, cross-legged, and sighed. He wasn't sure what "…consider what brought you here" meant.

Chapter Two:
Sewer Chase

The next day

Terry didn't sleep. The image of BGT getting shot played over in his head, mixed with memories of his drug-running days in Alberta. He saw visions of the time when he and his closest childhood friend were trapped in an alley during a fight. They were fortunately rescued, but not before three bullets tore through his friend's torso and one grazed his neck. His mind jumped between visions of carrying his friend's body out of the alley and carrying BGL.

He stood up from the bed and walked over to the window, opening the curtain to see a thin light that could have been a sign of sunrise. He watched for a few more minutes, but the light didn't change, prompting the thought that dawn wasn't coming. In his exhausted state, other possibilities didn't occur to him.

Terry was already in the bathroom when Katya woke up.

"I'll be out in a second," he called out. "Hey, while you're waiting, check and see if BrainMaze could make sense out of what we saw last night."

"Okay." She looked around for her Motif, finding it stuck in between the cushions of the sofa.

The display showed there was insufficient data to define the exact route connecting the sewer system in the temple to the central network. There were, however, huge gaps in the connections between old and new buildings.

She heard the bathroom door open, and Terry walked out with a towel wrapped around his waist and using another to dry his hair. "Anything?"

"Is that what you are wearing today?" She chuckled.

"Tempting, but not professional. What did BrainMaze find?"

"That we need more information to track where those Aliens came from. There are gaps in the system schematics." She showed her display to him with the missing segments.

"Aliens?" Terry gave her a puzzled look. "Is that what you think they are?"

Katya shook her head. "Not in the way you are thinking, but certainly alien as in 'not from around here'."

"Definitely agree there."

"Why do I not smell coffee?" Logan stumbled out of his room.

"Oh, geez, you definitely need it." Terry started walking toward the kitchen when Logan grabbed the towel he was wearing.

"Ah, perfect, I do need a towel." Logan smiled. "Terrance, please put some clothes on! There is a lady present!"

Terry snapped his other towel at Logan and walked to his room, laughing. "Make your own damn coffee."

"My, he's grumpy this morning." Logan tossed the wet towel aside and walked to the kitchen.

Katya was used to the playful banter of her colleagues and would usually engage, but she focused on the simulations.

"Logan, we will need to redo the analyses from last night's encounter. There are missing data."

Logan walked over and put his hand on her shoulder. "Coffee first, please. I can barely focus at the moment."

He walked over to the small refrigerator and took out a bottle of iced coffee.

Terry emerged from his room, dressed in surfing shorts and a t-shirt. "Are those gaps at the intersection of new and old infrastructure?"

Katya studied the schematics. "I believe so, but we need to confirm with Xi's staff today. I imagine they will have that information."

Logan guzzled the coffee and set it down on the table. "I will grab a quick shower now. Katya?"

"I showered last night, so I should be okay." She saw a message from Sara asking whether they were ready. "But hurry, please. The others are ready to go."

"On it! I'm on it!" Logan's voice trailed off as he entered the bathroom.

*****

"Did you have a pleasant evening?" Enrique greeted the team entering the complex.

"It was great, though we are all a little jet-lagged," Sara offered.

"Well, I am certain you will acclimate fast. The engineers are eager to meet with you as they have made some significant progress on the AI software." Enrique escorted them down the back corridor to the control room. "Two of your team are missing. The tall thin gentleman and the young lady, Yvette."

"The gentleman had to return home, and Yvette will not be working with us today," Baren answered.

The trio looked at one another. "Do you think he fired Yvette?" Terry whispered as they entered the control room.

The head engineer was in a far better mood on this day. "I am happy to report that we have been able to stabilize the local AI with a software patch."

"Great," Sara replied.

"Who sent you the patch?" TechStaff asked, knowing it likely did not come from Council HQ.

The head engineer raised one eyebrow. "I assumed you had provided the patch to update the system. When we checked it a few hours after you left, it was far more stable, and most of the areas of uncertainty were gone."

"I am glad the system is stable, but we didn't..." TechStaff was cut off.

"Super!" Katya exclaimed. "I am delighted our patch was successful. Logan, perhaps you or Terry could connect your Motif and double-check the stability?"

Logan wasn't sure what Katya was planning, but played along.

"Certainly." He walked over to the control panel and linked his Motif.

Katya turned to Terry and pulled him aside while Logan was setting up. "I think something is up here and don't completely trust the engineer. Let me set up a shadow link next to Logan's, and I will pull the data from the last 24 hours. I can analyze it in the background while you and Logan work with the engineers."

Terry nodded and went over to Logan. "Perhaps we could run a few tests on the current configuration to see how well the prediction landscape is working?"

Logan proceeded with his display projected to a large monitor. The local network schematics evolved much as they did the day before, except the uncertainty levels were considerably lower.

"There are a few areas where the probabilities are still in flux, but I suspect that will settle down in the next few hours as the programs adapt," Katya commented from the back of the room, as she registered the more volatile regions.

The analyses ran for another hour, at which point the volatility had settled and became random. Or at least, they appeared to be random.

"Throwing in random noise is precisely the strategy an adaptive system would use to evaluate new configurations." Katya watched the volatile regions move around the local network.

"We'll need to break soon," the head engineer interrupted. "Councillor Xi wants to talk with your team."

"Very well," Sara replied. "Hey, Professors, do you have enough data?"

Katya looked over at Logan, who nodded. "Yes, we are good for now."

Enrique escorted them to the Councillor's office. As they approached the door, Sara turned to him. "Could you find a place where the Professors can continue their work while we meet with Councillor Xi? I am sure their time would be better spent doing some analyses rather than listening to us talk politics."

"Of course, there is a conference room just down the hall." Enrique pointed and opened the Councillor's door. Xi was standing in the middle of the room, looking at a video feed.

"I see from the security cameras that you had a rather exciting visit to the new temple last night," Xi said in an odd tone that either conveyed humour or anger.

Sara looked back at the trio and whispered, "You three go on. We can handle this," and she pulled the door closed behind her.

The trio entered the conference room.

"Katya, what do you see in the new data?"

Before Terry could continue, Katya put her finger to her lips and put on her goggles. Logan and Terry did the same.

"I THINK WE WILL BE MONITORED IF WE SPEAK," she sent to her colleagues through their brain to speech (B2S) interface.

"WHAT DO YOU SEE IN THE ANALYSES?" Terry asked again.

"I THINK THE ALIENS MASK THEIR LOCATION NOW," came Katya's reply. "BUT MAY BE TESTING OUT NEW CONFIGURATIONS."

"THESE ARE THE VOLATILE REGIONS IN THE NETWORK," Logan added. "WE CAN TRIANGULATE TO SEE THE NEXT MOVE."

Terry spoke out loud, "I think we should revisit the place we went to last night. There is much more to see there, and I am certain that the origin of many of the problems comes from there."

"DISTRACTION," he then sent through his BrainMaze link to his colleagues.

Katya sent her analysis feed to Logan and Terry through the goggles, showing the local network with two new branches. One was in a mountain region and the other in a location near to where the group was staying.

"Perhaps when we get back to the flat tonight, we can go for a quick run. I am curious to explore the area around there," Katya said deliberately.

They continued the analyses when Enrique knocked on the door and entered. "The meeting with Councillor Xi is complete, and your friends are coming. May I bring you some refreshments?"

Sara, Baren and TechStaff walked into the room. Sara had an angry stare, and she looked over at Enrique. "I think we'll be fine. Please give us some time alone."

Sara closed the door. "Seems our trip to the temple was recorded by the security cameras on the street. They couldn't get the complete picture, especially the end, so I explained to Xi how we had an argument with the group inside the temple and could leave before anything bad happened." She let the comment sink in.

"Apparently, the congregation is heavily supported by the community because of their link to the green fluid. Many come to them to get cures for ailments, and some come to study to make a connection between the early religions and this supposedly magical green stuff.

"The community borders on fanatical in some cases and hired armed guards to protect their temple. It appears the congregation has relocated now, so the building is abandoned and no longer of interest to us."

She leaned forward and whispered, "I got the impression that Xi doesn't know about our 'new friends' who came out of the green slime."

"Still, I think it is worth checking the system there. We identified it just the other day, so I'd be interested to see how it was fixed so easily." Sara looked over at TechStaff. "Perhaps we could send someone over there?"

TechStaff looked up and nodded. "Yeah, sure. Nothing like seeing the actual site. I can get another sample of the green stuff. My reading of the sample I got last night said the stuff was harmless but has high salinity. That could be why is separates from the water, but I need more to be sure."

"Maybe the best option would be for the bodyguards to go there. You can take the Professors back to the hotel so they can finish their work in peace. Sebastian and I will hang back here. We can get a ride to the flat later and meet you there."

Terry raised his finger. "Shouldn't we go with them?"

Sara shook her head slightly. "I don't think that's wise. If they've cleaned the site, there won't be much to see, and given the aggression we saw last time, if there's anyone left there, I'd prefer to be cautious and leave it to the team members who are trained for this."

Terry gazed at her for a moment, not sure that she'd considered his past life and on-the-job training as a drug runner in Alberta.

Sara met his gaze as if to say, "I know what you're thinking, but let's not go there."

"We can use the electric motorcycles from the van." BGK looked over at Terry.

"We'll connect with you through the goggles when we are onsite."

"Why didn't anyone tell me we had electric motorcycles?" Logan shrugged.

The mid-afternoon vehicular traffic was light, and the street around the temple had only a few people walking about. The building was abandoned. Any sign of occupancy was effectively scrubbed, which included the bloodstains from BGT's wound.

The bodyguards turned their goggles on as they walked to the basement door, which was opened. BGK stayed at the top of the stairs to stand watch, while BGL descended with a weapon drawn.

The room was radically altered, with no obvious sign there

had been a pool.

BGL touched the ground. "This was just covered. The cement is damp."

She turned to go back upstairs. "We're going to check the water flow connection outside."

They left the building and went around the side to evaluate the water flow at the sewer. The flow appeared normal, with no evidence of green fluid.

"There's no one here, and the site has been scrubbed," BGL commented. "I think we'll head back to the hotel now unless there's something else you want us to check."

"No, go ahead. I don't think there's much else we can do there," TechStaff replied from inside the van.

She turned to the trio. "Someone made it look like nothing ever happened there."

Katya was looking out the window. "I have the feeling the Aliens may have left first, and then someone tried to cover up the fact they were there. I think Xi is hiding something or maybe working with them."

"You may be right, Katya, but I don't know what we are going to do at this moment." Logan tried to get her attention.

Katya looked down at her Motif and the mapping of the new branches. "Well, I don't know about you, but I would like to get a run in tonight, so once we get back to our flat, let's go before Sara and the others arrive."

TechStaff laughed. "Your reputation for running addiction is quite accurate. I think I will pass on the run, but I can get us back to our flat."

Katya sent a B2S message to Terry and Logan. "ANOTHER IDEA. THERE IS A WATER DISTRIBUTION STATION CLOSE

TO OUR HOTEL. IT'S A MAJOR INTERSECTION, SO MAYBE WE CAN TRACK MORE FROM THERE."

Katya glanced at Terry, nodded, and looked at Logan.

"I GUESS YOU MEAN THAT THE THREE OF US GO OUT ALONE?" Logan sent back.

Terry smiled and raised his eyebrows.

TechStaff noticed Terry's expression. "What are you two scheming?"

"Just planning a running route." Katya took off her goggles.

Jumping in deep

TechStaff sent a message to Sara and Baren that they had arrived at their flat.

"Sara says they'll be here in about an hour, so that should give you time for your run."

"Super." Katya jumped out of the vehicle and turned to Terry and Logan. "Let's meet back here in 10 minutes, and bring your goggles, too. It will help if it gets too dark."

The initial pace for the run was slow, with Terry taking the lead, scanning the surroundings to identify the water distribution network. Terry remembered a paper on old architecture for water distribution, which warned of a weakness in the system. He had pulled the paper up on his Motif and used this new information to build another simulation. Within seconds, BrainMaze had pinpointed the single point in the system that was most vulnerable.

Terry signaled a turn and ran to a nondescript building that had the sewer system access point. The door was unlocked.

The trio descended the stairs among the enormous steel pipes and rusting turbines. Terry spotted the weak point several flights of stairs below.

"You see?" he said. "Where that green sludge comes in, the filters only deal with large particles. It's easy for it to diffuse through the system here without detection."

As Logan watched the rising green tide, his heart raced, as he knew what might be coming. "Let's get back up the top," Terry said. "This green stuff will flood the chamber soon, and we don't want to be swimming in it."

As the three emerged, a large Alien in white clothing ran toward them.

"I see a gun!" Katya shouted.

The trio ducked behind a fence, but not before the Alien had fired a warning shot.

Terry looked over the fence to see the Alien jump into the sewer. "It's going in!" he said.

Logan acted. "I will go in after it." He stood up. "We were going to have to go in anyway, and I did some bog diving when I was a Ph.D. student. It took me a year to get over the trauma and at least that long to clean my glasses." With that and a smile, Logan leaped over the fence and ran into the sewer after the Alien.

When Logan came to the first landing, he paused, kneeling to get his goggles out and rearrange his gear. The dim light from the sewer was enough for him to do this without needing more light and attracting attention. As he knelt, he scanned around to see any signs of the Alien. Other than the sight and sound of the green sludge pouring into the chamber, he could detect nothing. He put the goggles on and waited. *Katya, how do I look?* he thought.

The trio had discussed a routine for situations like this. They were vulnerable, with one person separated from the group, but the goggles provided an interface with BrainMaze that allowed them to continue to work as a team, even at a distance. Terry and Katya watched Logan disappear and proceeded with their duties. Katya immediately put on her goggles and recalibrated her BrainMaze interface to link with Logan's. Terry stood watch in case other threats emerged.

He glanced at the B2S icon in his goggles and thought again, *Katya, how do I look?*

Katya scanned her display. She saw her avatar sync up and then the feed from Logan's link: "KATYA, HOW DO I LOOK?" The B2S converter was on silent text-only mode, given the precarious situation they were in.

Katya scanned the readings from Logan's avatar, smiled and thought, *Logan, you look hungry and a little hungover.*

Soon the response came: "KATYA." Even without sound, she could image the drawn-out vowels feigning disapproval of her comment. Of course, the B2S converter was not perfect, so who knew how her thought was actually translated?

"LOGAN, YOU LOOK HAIRY AND A LITTLE HAWAIIAN," was the read-out Logan saw on his display and chuckled under his breath. *I guess that means I am okay*, he thought to himself.

He stood and saw a shadow behind him. He knew this was in a dangerous position, but rather than turning, which would waste precious milliseconds, he stayed low, kicked his leg out to the side and swung it around behind to trip the shadow. As he turned around, gratified that his body allowed this defensive move, he swept the legs from under the Alien. The leg sweep was enough to unbalance it, sending it tumbling sideways toward the edge of the walkway. This gave Logan enough time to get himself upright and face the Alien. For now, at least, he felt he had the advantage.

Terry had not been paying attention to Katya while he scanned the area. He resisted putting on his goggles, knowing he would feel tempted to follow Logan through the sewer rather than keep watch, but his attention snapped immediately to Katya when she let out an audible gasp. He backed closer to her, keeping his ears open.

"He turned quickly and now is fixating in front. I think he engaged the Alien," she whispered.

Logan didn't know what to do next. He could attack, which is what his training compelled him to do, or he could wait and see. The best approach was to capture and contain the Alien, so that they could figure out their intentions.

The Alien did not rise. Instead, it rolled off the walkway down to the green sludge below.

Damn, I wasn't planning on a swim tonight, Logan joked to himself. He glanced at the B2S icon and thought: "Katya, it's gone into the green. I am going after it."

Logan ran down to the next level, where the green sludge had risen. Fortunately, his neoprene boots would work well here, so he locked his weapon and holstered it as he entered the green. He fitted a mask over his mouth and nose to shield against any toxins in the green sludge.

Rather than sludge, in the typical sense, it was more like slightly thick green water. It was mostly translucent, so Logan could make out the motions of the Alien as it moved deeper into the green. Its motions were erratic; perhaps Logan's leg sweep had injured it.

"LOGAN, WE MAY HAVE TROUBLE READING YOU IN THE GREEN. BE CAREFUL, AND KEEP YOUR CAMERA ACTIVE."

Logan acknowledged the message to himself and slipped into the green. It was deep, requiring using some techniques his wife taught him about free diving and breath control. He tried to relax his diaphragm and keep relaxed as he sunk farther down. About 10 metres away, he could see the Alien, still showing the same erratic movements.

Logan drifted forward slowly, but stopped when he saw the Alien's body split into pieces. Each piece morphed slightly in the green to become mobile and began moving toward Logan. Dirty buggers, he thought as backed away and tried to ascend to the walkway.

When complex systems face a challenge, they send out multiple agents to try different solutions to address that challenge. The immune system is a perfect example of this, where numerous antibodies can be mobilized to face a new intruder, and the ones that are more effective are reproduced. Through this, the system can adapt to the new intruder and have an effective defence the next time an intruder is encountered.

"Terry, Logan is in trouble. You need to get down there fast. I will get help," Katya said aloud as she turned to see that Terry had already gone.

Terry turned on his goggle display to see what Logan's camera showed. When he saw the Alien roll into the green rather than standing to face Logan, it occurred to him that the green might provide access to a regressive state for the Aliens — a sort of "safe place". When the Alien split into segments, this reminded him of a bifurcation, wherein the system hits a trigger point, and then new configurations are accessible. The green may provide that stable state from which the Aliens could try new configurations.

Rather than going into the sewer, Terry decided the best way to combat them was to eliminate the stable state and thereby eliminate the options. He ran to an access door down from the sewer where the controls for water flow were housed. There, he reversed the flow, hoping that it would pull the green out of the sewer.

Terry activated his goggles, glanced at the B2S icon, and thought: *Logan, hold on to something quickly."* Within a few seconds, "OKAY" appeared on Terry's display, and he started the reverse flow procedure. He glanced at Logan's camera feed to see the Alien's progression toward him had stopped. Terry ran to the sewer to get down to Logan.

Logan saw the message from Terry and was holding tight to the submerged stair rail, all the while watching the pieces of the dismembered creature drifting toward him. Their flow stopped, and Logan felt the reversal of the green sludge as it was pulled into the drain. As the fluid continued to drain, some of the Alien's segments moved randomly in different directions, as if testing an alternative path. The last of the green drained, and the segments slowly reformed until all that was left was the intact Alien body on the sewer floor.

Chapter Three:
Alien dissection

Recon

Logan stared at the Alien, waiting for movement. He released his grip on the rail and heard Terry calling him. "Logan, you good?"

"Yeah, all good." Logan felt pain in his elbow from the strain of fighting the reversed flow. It was the same elbow he damaged on his bike trip in the hills behind his home. Katya ran to the sewer entrance next to Terry. "Kim and Sebastian are on the way. Sara is bringing a vehicle, too, I think."

"Okay, I'll go down to Logan to make sure he's alright." Terry sprinted down the stairwell.

He stopped one level above when he saw Logan approaching the body on the floor. Logan walked around it, stopped at its head, and looked up at Terry. "I can't tell if it's alive or dead, or even if it's real."

Terry leaped down to the floor and scanned the area to make sure it was safe. Logan fixated on the body.

"What was up with the floating segments?" Terry focused on the body now.

"I honestly don't know. I think the green medium is a catalyst that allows them to recombine. We probably should try to get a sample to analyze it in more detail. We thought it's just slime, but there's a lot we are missing." Logan knelt down, taking his gloves off.

Terry walked up to Logan and tapped his shoulder. "No touching, eh? You don't know where it's been."

Logan smiled at Terry, then reached his hand forward to touch the head of the body. It felt artificial.

Nothing happened.

Logan scanned the body and spied a place on the torso where there remained some of the green. He placed his hand there. His scientific curiosity and excitement were stronger than the fear.

The body surface under Logan's hand moved up and around his fingers and hand.

Logan pulled back. "That is cool."

"Only a scientist would say that," came the voice of BGL from above them, as she descended the stairs.

Logan stood quickly and backed away from the body. "I was testing a hypothesis!"

"Of course, you were." BGL came down the last stairs, followed by TechStaff and BGK.

TechStaff knelt to scrutinize the body and looked up at Logan and Terry. "So, we can't examine it here in case the locals show up. We brought a body bag that was in the medical supply crate. Can we carry it up in that?"

"I have a feeling we will need to put something around it. Also, we need to get some of the green stuff collected so that we can examine it too." Logan pointed to the drain where there was a small pool of green.

"The bag is heavy rubber," BGL commented as she unfolded it. "Do you think that would be enough?"

"I think so, but let's rig up something for extra reinforcement. Maybe we can use a wood plank." Logan looked around to see if there was anything appropriate, but saw nothing.

"Logan, it will be easier if we winch it up out of the sewer and put in on a board up there. If we use a regular rope, I think we will be okay," Terry said, as he looked up to the door at the top of the stairs.

He connected to Katya. "CAN YOU SEND DOWN A ROPE?"

Katya read the message and thought for a moment. "ARE YOU TOO LAZY TO CLIMB BACK UP?"

She could hear muffled laughter from the sewer. She turned to see Sara arriving in a large vehicle. "They need a rope."

Sara blinked for a moment, frowned, and looked directly at Katya. "I am trying to stay calm here, Katya. Do you know how incredibly stupid your group's solo trek was? You've seen what these creatures and their entourage can do, yet you go out without your bodyguards? We can't afford to lose anyone else."

Sara's tone put Katya off-balance. "I know, and I am sorry for this. But let's not argue this now, okay? We have captured one of the creatures, and we can study it to understand what we are up against. I know our methods may not be the most elegant, Sara, but please trust that we produce good outcomes."

Sara shook her head and turned to go back to the vehicle. "We have nylon rope. Will that do?"

"Yes, of course, thank you." Katya walked over to Sara. "I know this is incredibly stressful, Sara. Please be assured that we are here for you."

Sara still felt anger looking at Katya, but maintained her composure. "Thanks, Katya. This whole thing is tough on us all. Let's get this thing out of here before someone sees us."

Katya took the rope and went into the sewer to the first landing. She looked down to see the team standing next to the body with the body bag unfolded next to it. "I have rope. I can let it down when you are ready."

"Okay, so how are we going to do this?" Logan rubbed his hands together as he circled the body. He looked over to Terry, who was suctioning the green into a rubber insulated flask. "I see you are busy, Terry."

Terry turned his head. "Our gloves are insulated, remember? You can probably wrap the bag around it and scoop to get it in. Besides, you touched it already and are still here to talk to us."

Logan pursed his lips, miming, "Shhh," and TechStaff snapped her head around to look at him. "Did you take your glove off? That's crazy!"

"This is what you get when you send a theoretician out to do fieldwork." Logan shrugged.

Terry laughed and walked over to the body, placing the flask in a pouch and signaling to BGK and BGL. "You two get the bag lined up parallel, and let's see if we can stuff it in with minimal trouble. I don't have a spatula that big, unfortunately."

"Ah, you scientists are hopeless." TechStaff moved in front. "This is like moving a body on a bed when the person is unconscious. You wrap, lift and wrap." She motioned.

Terry stood back and let TechStaff in. She knelt as BGK and BGT pulled the bag around the Alien without touching it. She motioned to count to three, and, on three, they lifted the Alien into the bag and pulled the rest of the surrounding material.

"It's deceptively light," BGT said as he stood.

"That's concerning." Terry looked around the sewer again. "I wonder if because it's disconnected, its mass is actually less. The ones we encountered the other day seemed very substantial. Wrapping a rope around the bag to haul it up may damage it."

"WE NEED SOMETHING TO HAUL IT UP. TOO FRAGILE,"

flashed across Katya's goggles.

Katya called out to Sara. "They need something to haul it up."

Sara went back to the vehicle. "We have a foldable gurney." She pulled out a large case and took out the gurney, assembling it on the road.

Katya saw some people gathering. "Sara, where is Baren?"

"Here," Baren said as he ran up to the vehicle. "Sorry, it took me a while to get out of the meeting, and I did not want to appear rude. Is Yvette here?"

"No, we did not contact her." Katya looked at Baren. "Is she part of the team now?"

"Yes, of course, she is! She has valuable technical skills that we need for this." Baren sounded exasperated by the question.

"I see." Katya paused. "You can let her know where we are, but I don't think we can stay here much longer." She pointed to the small group forming around them.

"Need your help here, Sebastian," Sara called as she pulled the gurney to the sewer door.

They carried the gurney into the sewer and set it down on the first landing. Katya wrapped the rope about the midsection, tied it and lowered it.

Terry watched the orange gurney float down to them. He glanced at the body bag and felt an odd pang of sorrow, like he was witnessing a friend being taken away.

BGK and BGL pulled the gurney close to the bag, loosened the rope, and gently placed the bag on the gurney. They fixed the straps on the gurney to secure the bag and reattached the rope.

Katya saw BGK give the thumbs up. "Okay, pull it up." She watched as Terry guided the ascent, making sure the gurney did not hit against rails. Terry waved to the team below to come up.

TechStaff looked around. "Let's go. I think we have everything. I will set a timer for five minutes to flood the chamber so that there is no evidence left."

The team ran up the stairs and got to the landing as Sara and Baren pulled the gurney from below and walked to the exit.

A barrage of flashing lights greeted them at the door.

"Secretary Baren, who's in the bag?"

"Secretary Baren, is this how the Global Council negotiates now?"

The outside was crowded with members of the press, shining lights as they captured videos of Baren and Sara taking the gurney out. Sara was far enough away from the light that she was not recognizable.

BGK emerged from the sewer and placed himself firmly between the press mob and Baren. Baren motioned to BGL to take the gurney from him.

"My friends," Baren said as he stepped in front of BGK and raised his hands to call attention to himself. "There has been a tragedy here today with our team of engineers."

Baren tried to draw the crowd away from the vehicle.

"As you know, our mission was to update the water system to better protect you from floods during the rainy season." Baren motioned to TechStaff to step up.

"One of our engineers was working in this water exchange station and, unfortunately, the station was flooded without warning. I wish we could say that we saved her, but sadly, we were not in time."

"Who was she, Secretary Baren? What was she trying to do in there?"

"I am sure you understand that I cannot tell you these things.

We need to contact her family, and, given the circumstances that led to her death, I do not want to say much more until I have spoken to local authorities." Baren watched as the body was loaded into the vehicle. Sara quickly jumped inside, followed by BGK and BGL. Katya remained by the door as Terry and Logan stood just inside. "Kim, can you please tell these people a bit about what happened?"

"WHEN KIM TAKES THE ATTENTION, YOU MUST MOVE," flashed across Katya's goggles. *This must have come from Baren*, she thought. *When did he get access to the B2S system?*

TechStaff stepped next to Baren. "Hi, my name is Kim. Uh, some people call me TechStaff." She smiled shyly. "As the Secretary said, we were looking at the system and testing the water flow when the feeder system blew, and the chamber flooded." There was a noticeable quiver in her voice.

"I ran when it burst, but then I saw my friend was trapped and," she trailed off and bowed her head.

All but one of the vehicle's doors was closed now.

Baren put his arm around TechStaff's shoulder. "I am sorry to cut this short, but we must leave so that I can take care of my team. I will arrange a full press conference for tomorrow morning. I trust you will respect the privacy of my team and our fallen colleague until then." Baren guided TechStaff toward the vehicle.

"Secretary Baren, have you informed the Chair of this tragedy?"

Baren paused and glanced back. "I can assure you she is fully aware of the situation." The door of the vehicle closed.

Baren blew out a long sigh, sitting back in his seat. The press focused the lights on the vehicle to see who else was inside.

TechStaff started Phantom Mode for the vehicle, blocking their view.

The sewer chamber burst with water again, perfectly on cue, and the press ran to investigate.

"Remind me to give you a big raise," Baren said to TechStaff.

"Remind me to give you a big raise," Sara said to Baren. "That was an amazing performance, both of you! I just hope Xi and his group don't get too worked up about this. I doubt they are going to like the idea of us poking around in their sewer systems after what happened in the temple the other day."

Baren finished composing a message. "We will explain ourselves soon. I sent a message to Xi that we are coming to their office now with an urgent matter and sent the link to the press feed. It is the only place here that we can examine the creature without being disturbed."

"Great idea, Sebastian." Sara saw a copy of the message Baren sent along with the video feed from the press. The video was sufficiently erratic that it was practically impossible to identify any of the team, except for Baren and TechStaff.

Katya watched behind them as they pulled away, seeing some press members trying to follow their vehicle.

She turned to Baren. "Was that you who sent the communication via the B2S system?"

Baren removed his glasses. "Ah, yes, I borrowed these from Yvette, since she wasn't using them."

Katya frowned and looked at Logan, who shrugged.

"I am surprised you trained it so well," she continued.

"Well, I think that is more a reflection of how well you've built your system rather than some heroic effort on my part." Baren grinned and turned his attention to the vehicle console to track their progress to Xi's office compound.

Some explaining to do

Xi watched as the large vehicle pulled up to the front of their office. He motioned for them to drive into the open garage and followed them in as the vehicle parked.

BGL and BGK were the first to exit the vehicle, followed by Sara and Baren.

"I'm sorry for this interruption." Sara approached Xi. "As you saw on the news, there's been a bit of an incident. We have a lot to explain."

Xi nodded and looked at Baren. "I could have sent my staff to assist you in the sewer system with no question. Now I understand that one of your staff may have drowned in there because you went alone."

"Not exactly," Baren grimaced. "I think it may be better to show you first and then explain."

Baren opened the rear hatch of the vehicle and, with the help of BGK, pulled the gurney out, setting it down. The rest of the team gathered around.

"Could one of you show us the contents of the bag?" Baren motioned toward the trio.

Terry shrugged. "Sure." He put on his gloves and unzipped the bag.

The Alien looked more formless than when it was first placed in the bag, almost as if it were deflating. There were large clusters of white interposed with black, and some gaps were forming.

"What is this?" Xi gasped, looking down.

"We are not completely sure, Councillor. We came across a group of these the other day at the temple, and, well, let's just say they do not appear to be friendly," Baren responded first.

Logan was preparing to say something, and Sara caught his eye, indicating he should stay quiet.

She spoke next. "We believe these creatures are part of what is causing some of the problems your group has encountered in the water system."

"This does not look like a creature. This looks more like some sort of Alien or robot." Xi tried to get a closer look. He reached out to touch it.

BGK grabbed Xi's hand. "Probably not a good idea. We haven't assessed whether they are contagions."

Xi stood slowly to keep his eyes fixed on the Alien. "I understand. Chair Meyer, there is a room in the basement that you can use to examine this. Do you need any assistance? I can contact some of our scientists if you think it necessary."

"Thank you, but our three colleagues will be enough for now. I also have a degree in molecular biology, so we have more than enough scientists at the moment." Sara paused. "Do you have a secure video link we can use? It may be helpful for us to connect with an old friend who is an expert in biological networks."

"Of course. Please follow me, and I will take you to the room." Xi gestured and walked toward a door at the back of the garage. "I would like to be present during your examination. This is my jurisdiction, and if these creatures are a threat, I need to know about it." His tone was slightly adversarial.

"I was going to suggest exactly that," Baren said calmly as he motioned to BGL and BGK to lift the gurney.

Sara glanced at Baren and back at Xi. "If you can set up a comm block as soon as possible, that would be helpful too. Now that everyone knows we are here, there'll be people trying to hack in to see what we are up to."

Noisy Fractals

Xi led them to a large service elevator that descended into the basement. As they exited, Baren's device vibrated.

Baren looked at his device and then at Xi. "Yvette is here. I will go back up and fetch her while you get my colleagues set up."

"Do you know the codes for the door?" Xi prepared to write them on a piece of paper.

"Of course! I have them from our meeting earlier today." Baren closed the elevator doors and ascended.

"He's an odd one." Xi shook his head.

"He is quirky but effective, Councillor." Sara grinned and started down the hall.

Xi ran ahead of the group and unlocked double doors at the end of the corridor. The large room contained several long tables and workstations. "We were using this as a computer lab at one point, but moved the lab to another part of the building. The space is secure, and few come down here anymore, so we should not be disturbed."

TechStaff set her gear bag down and looked back at BGK. "Let's put it down over on the big table. I'll set up the video link from here, and we can connect one set of goggles to project the video stream."

Katya was utterly lost in thought and realized she had said nothing since they arrived. She looked over to Terry and Logan, who were talking with Sara. She looked down at her Motif and saw that she had no connection to BrainMaze. "Are we no longer able to connect outside with the comm block?"

Xi turned to Katya. "Correct. This is what you asked for."

"Sure, but if we are going to do this examination properly, we will need to link with BrainMaze." Katya held up her Motif.

"I think we can piggyback it on the line for the video link. I don't imagine we'll be moving massive amounts of data." TechStaff began setting up the connections.

Sara walked over to TechStaff. "Espinoza will be online in a few minutes. He's 12 hours behind us, so it's early afternoon there."

"Espinoza?" Katya asked.

"Yeah, Osborn Espinoza. He and I worked together when I was still doing science. He's an expert in biological networks. We were studying the interactions of genetic and protein networks before I changed careers and got into policy and politics."

Katya raised her eyebrows. "Impressive. And you also found time for military training during all that?"

"Actually, that was before I went to university. I was considering going into the military, but I found the framework too restrictive. I got reprimanded a bunch of times for not following protocol, and whenever I would ask why things were done in a certain way, they'd usually say that's the way it's always been done. I don't mind following someone, but I have to believe in them."

Katya smiled. "I understand completely."

Logan walked up to the table and carefully unzipped the bag. The Alien continued to flatten, almost like liquid metal. "Can we cut the bag open? I am afraid it's getting more fragile as it sits and don't want it to break apart anymore."

BGK pulled out a large knife and carefully split the top and bottom of the bag, opening it like a sheet. The release of tension allowed the Alien's components to spread out even more, giving it a two-dimensional appearance.

"It's as if there is nothing to keep the pieces together." Terry pointed to the gaps — breaks in the body where they could see through to the black bag.

"The green fluid appears to have some effect that may bind them." Logan pointed at the few areas where a bit of the green remained, along with the cohesion of the white and black segments.

Terry grabbed the flask of the green sample he had taken from the sewer. He opened it and siphoned off a small amount, bending over the torso of the Alien. "Let me try a little here." He dripped the green on a patch.

Nothing happened.

"I don't get it. When you touched it in the sewer, the thing's skin tried to merge with you." Terry peered at Logan.

"If it's a catalyst, it needs something to catalyze. Maybe we need an energy source." Logan looked back at Katya. "Do you have any of those stimulation electrodes with you?"

Katya stepped toward them. "Yes, why do you ask?"

Logan pointed at the green patch Terry dropped on the Alien. "I think we need a bit of a kick to enable the green stuff to have any effect. The elements on its body could be like sets of coupled oscillators, but there is no momentum. If we inject some signal, the green might transmit it throughout and activate them."

"Interesting idea." Katya looked at the green liquid. She reached into her bag and pulled out two small circle electrodes connected to a wireless transmitter. These were a prototype for brain stimulation that interfaced with BrainMaze to help bias brain network configurations for her BCI platform.

"How shall we do this?" She held the electrodes up.

Logan pointed at the torso. "Well, let's put the electrodes at opposite ends of the green stuff and send a few small pulses. You can do that without a BrainMaze headset, right?"

"Yes, I can control the pulse generator from my Motif." Katya carefully placed the electrode in the green.

Katya stepped back and sent a single square-wave. "This will be five milliseconds."

Nothing happened.

She increased the amplitude slightly and sent another pulse.

Nothing happened.

"Maybe try a short pulse train, Katya. I don't think these single pulses are enough to get the system out of the dormant state." Logan looked closer at the green and stepped back.

Katya sent a stream of 10 pulses. "Ah, now we get some action."

The individual white and black segments began slow oscillations, moving toward each other, then away.

Katya set the system to send 20 pulses.

The segments followed the same dance, moving toward each other but never touching.

Terry considered what he was observing. "I think the pulses are too simple. If this is a complex system, we should try a noise pulse. The small chaos that gets into the system may be enough to give the system more configurations to explore. The simple pulses enable only one configuration."

"Okay." Katya made a few adjustments. "I will use a white noise pulse with half the amplitude of the simple waves."

The effect was immediate, but brief. The segments moved in a similar oscillatory fashion, with some touching and exchanging elements.

"Let me try with a higher amplitude."

The convergence and divergence pattern was more persistent now and distributed across more segments that were under the green fluid.

"I think I will stop here," Katya said. "We can try to map out response space here, but I fear that if we get too far along the noise curve, we may not be able to control the response."

"We're likely to map what's called a stochastic resonance curve for signal detection in the presence of noise." Terry drew an inverted-U in the air. "That's where the noise effect is weak at low levels, peaks as the noise amplitude increases and then drops again once the amplitude goes too high."

"True, but we don't know what the response on the tail-end of the curve will be. I'd be more comfortable doing this in my lab, where I have better instruments to measure stimulus-response behaviour." Katya lifted the electrodes from the torso.

"Don't you guys ever wait for anyone?" Sara walked up behind them.

Katya turned, stuffing the electrodes into her pouch. "Sorry, we are not usually this out of control, I assure you. It's a combination of excitement and sleep deprivation."

"I get it." Sara held up her device, showing a video image. "This is Professor Espinoza, whom I mentioned to you earlier. Say hi everyone."

The trio waved, and Espinoza, looking exactly the stereotype of old professor with an unruly grizzled beard and hair, held up his hand in greeting. "Ozzy, please. Let's not be so formal. Terry, Logan and Katya, I am happy to finally meet you. I have been following your work for some time. What an exciting moment for us to start a collaboration!"

"Great to meet you as well, Ozzy," Terry responded. "Your work has been central to my thinking on network analytics!"

"Okay, okay, enough with the love fest," Sara gently interrupted. "It's really late here, and we need to get a few hours of sleep, so let's jump right into it, okay?"

Back on task

Baren entered the code to open the door and saw Yvette standing, slightly out of breath.

"Sorry it took so long." She puffed. "I had a hard time extracting Logan's video record of the sewer. I think after the last hack into BrainMaze, they're updating their security more frequently."

"This is why you are so important to the team, Yvette." Baren motioned for her to enter and closed the door. They started walking toward the elevator.

"The others have started to examine the creature, and they are connecting with a colleague overseas. You should be able to patch into that feed to capture the data." Baren punched in the code in the elevator.

They both entered, and as the elevator descended, Baren pressed the STOP button and turned to Yvette. "I know you have a history with Logan, but it is very important to be professional. We have established a trusting partnership with the Professors, and I suspect we will get to a critical junction soon. I need to know I can rely on you."

Yvette clenched her jaw and looked down for a moment. She had an enviable position working in the Global Council. She withheld her reflexive response, knowing her temper could get her in trouble. If they were successful in this current project, she would be comfortable for life. She looked directly into Baren's eyes. "There is no one you can count on more than me."

Baren nodded, turned, pressed the GO button, and the elevator continued its descent.

They entered the room just as the video projection of Ozzy was cast into the room from Sara's device.

"Ah, hello, Professor Espinoza." Baren waved as he walked to the image. "I am Sebastian, and behind me is Yvette."

"Ozzy, please. We're all friends here." Espinoza turned his gaze toward the table.

"So, this is your Alien? Well, it's definitely not organic in the sense that we usually consider it. It has disintegrated too quickly for it to be purely biological."

"How do you mean?" Katya looked at the video.

"Most biological systems have multiple levels of organization that help to keep the system together if there is injury. Even after you die, the body stays relatively intact. This creature appears to have decayed quite rapidly, which suggests that the multiscale coherence does not go as deep."

Espinoza looked over at Sara. "I saw the video feed from the sewer. Quite an amazing transformation. I'm glad you didn't get sucked in, Logan."

Logan raised his eyebrows, nodding in confirmation.

"Ozzy, one thing we noticed is that the white and black units in these organisms seem to have slightly different behaviours. The white ones are more numerous and quite volatile, while the black ones move slower," Katya spoke up.

Espinoza looked over at Katya. "Well, you are the brain scientists, but it looked to me like the white ones are excitatory and inhibitory units, from what I have seen in the videos."

"Ah, good observation!" Katya glanced back at the table. "But then why would they move around if they were modelling the E/I balance of the brain?"

Espinoza cocked his head. "E/I balance?"

Katya turned back to the video. "Sorry, excitation/inhibition balance. I forget how often we assume everyone understands our jargon."

"There is another way to consider this," Espinoza continued. "Different complex systems may employ similar strategies to achieve a certain outcome. I mean strategies generally, like power-law scaling, fractal patterns, multiscale organization, nonlinearity, et cetera. This E/I balance might represent such a strategy that the brain uses, and maybe these organisms have as well."

Logan stepped up. "Can we take a moment to review the video feeds? I would particularly like to see how these black and white elements are moving." He glanced at TechStaff. "I'd like to patch this through BrainMaze to look at the dynamic features."

"No problem." TechStaff made a few adjustments. "You can do this through your Motif thing, I assume?"

Logan confirmed. "Probably." He configured the analysis of the dynamics.

The video feeds cycled through different magnifications and playback speeds of the Aliens. At the first encounter in the temple, they noted slight variation between individuals in the proportion of white and black elements that each one had. Logan pointed out the subtle differences in the limbs. At a faster playback, they showed variations in the location and density of the elements. Logan zoomed out, showing a similar variation across the Aliens, where there appeared to be momentary synchrony as the white and black elements moved across them.

Logan then played the video from the sewer. He tracked the separation of the segments from the Alien's body, noting each maintained a similar proportion of white and black elements, though within a segment, the relative locations would shift. As the segments reconnected, the elements could interchange and break apart again.

"These are like modules," Logan commented as he paused the playback. "Having these modules means there is some exchangeability and redundancy in the system that allows for more efficient configurations. There's a fable from Herb Simon about the two watchmakers, Tempus and Hora, where Tempus pre-assembles little modules of watch pieces that can be used in any watch. The modular organization enables him to build many watches by focusing on building blocks and also makes the construction robust to interruption. Hora builds his watches piece-by-piece, so when interrupted, he has to start over again."

Terry interjected. "There's a link to the brain here. Our cortex has this sort of modularity too. There are collections of cells that form columns that are similar to each other. Well, spatially, in the sense that those close together show a similar structure. It's almost plug-and-play. These modules don't move around, but they can show subtle variations in their function that depend on how they interact with their immediate neighbours."

The video continued showing the separation of segments into smaller, similarly structured white and black collectives.

"Got it." Logan paused the playback again and sent a graph of the results to the video display.

"So, it seems you're right, Ozzy and Katya, that the white and black elements are mimicking something like excitatory and inhibitory units. But here is the important thing — they act on different spatial scales."

The graph showed connections between the white segments, which were dense and local. The connections between black segments were spread farther apart, yet each black element was also connected with the white elements in its immediate location. Logan moved a slider that changed the timestamp for the graph and showed how the connections between the distant black elements would change more slowly and inhibit the local white nodes.

Katya marvelled at this. "It appears that the white excitatory nodes establish a local dynamic, which is followed by a diffuse burst from the black nodes that puts a limit on the local dynamic. The cool thing is that these black nodes interact over quite some distance, which somehow coordinates their inhibitory volleys."

Logan approached the display, pointing to the movement of the black nodes. "Yes, and I think these elements work on different spatial and temporal scales. The white ones are fast and local, the black ones slower and more distributed."

Logan set the video of the sewer scene into motion again, having Terry's graph analytics tracking the node actions at the same time. The scene moved to the portion where the Alien segments got closer to him, almost touching. Logan focused the analysis on the segments that were closest to him in the video. The graph analysis showed an increase in the speed of white excitatory node interactions, with a parallel rise in the strength of the interactions between black inhibitory nodes.

"They are close to a bifurcation," Logan spoke. "Though it is not clear what the next configuration would be."

The video then showed the green fluid being retracted. The excitatory nodes continued their rapid interactions, but the effect of inhibitory nodes abruptly reduced. The excitatory interactions decoupled, becoming even more local. The video moved to the portion where Logan grabbed the railing as the suction from the drain pulled at him.

"It's as if the inhibitory nodes are acting like a slowly moving influence that enables the excitatory nodes to move around in different configurations at a faster timescale. Removing the green fluid probably disrupted the global coupling, and the system collapsed." Logan rubbed his elbow on the arm that he used to grasp the railing in the video.

Travel back to HQ

Espinoza, having considered the video, offered a new perspective. "I'm thinking about some work I started a while ago, looking at how different time scales can interact in coordinating behaviour."

The group turned their attention to him.

"These organisms may be the embodiment of such a principle."

Espinoza continued. "It is trivial for me to say this because any complex adaptive system will show these principles, but these organisms are engineered specifically on overt principles in a way that takes their physical capabilities to a new level.

"Consider this. It is far more efficient to establish modules that carry some rudimentary function and put them together so that their interactions have a much broader capacity than any one module alone. As I understand it, in the brain, these would be like the cortical columns Terry mentioned."

Katya interjected. "So you're saying that if I hook up cortical columns to the eyes, they become visual cortex, but if I hook them up to the ears, they become auditory cortex? I thought that theory was passé?"

"You mean 'equipotentiality'?" Terry answered. "Like most things in science, theories fall in and out of favour. When Karl Lashley proposed the concept in the 1930s, it was more in response to the observation that he couldn't identify a single part of the brain that contained something like a memory. You train a rat in a maze, then lesion the part of the brain that supposedly learned the specifics of the maze, but you can't. At least, that was what he reported. The idea was misinterpreted over the years, I think, to suggest that Lashley didn't believe there was the localization of function, which was not the case. Equipotentiality was really the idea that other brain regions could compensate for the loss of others, to a point. If there is too much damage, there will be a loss of function."

"Exactly, Terry," Espinoza continued. "And at that time, the principles of complex adaptive systems were not developed, so there was no framework that allowed for adaptation of the system. These systems have a natural redundancy built-in that gives a great deal of flexibility and robustness. You may recall that most modern work considers the cortical column as the basic module for the brain."

Sara frowned. "I'm losing you here. How does this relate to our friend on the table?"

"These black and white units in the Alien function like equipotential cortical columns. It's not entirely 'hot-swappable' in that you can't take a module that's in the foot and put it in the face, but locally, you can. For these things, the interplay of the black and white elements sculpts the functions of the module." Espinoza looked to the side to recall something. "Can we look at the log from the temple again?"

TechStaff reran the video from the moment the first organism emerged from the green liquid.

"Let's step this part along in two-second jumps," Logan suggested.

The second and third one emerged. Then the first reached back into the green and extracted one more. Espinoza called out, "Pause," as another organism was extracted.

"Look at the differences in black and white densities across these organisms. Terry, can you quantify this?"

"No problem." Terry entered a few commands into the console. About 10 seconds later, a ratio showing the rough proportion of visible black and white elements on each organism was displayed next to it. Some were greater than one, indicating more white, and other were less than one, indicating more black.

"Step forward now, one frame at a time," Espinoza continued.

TechStaff advanced the video. Whenever one organism touched another, their ratios would change.

"They're like cells." Sara watched the numbers change. "Or bacteria exchanging vesicles so that the information that one organism has is passed to the rest."

Espinoza nodded. "That's my hunch, too. From our perspective, we tend to think of our own bodies as the highest autonomous unit. We are made up of billions of cells that have evolved to serve different functions, and each interacts to adapt as we grow. We don't consider that this co-development could also happen between bodies because we can't think past the scale of our own bodies."

Terry rubbed his chin. "I think I see where you are going with this."

"We rarely think of how we influence each other collectively, but that's been shown time and time again in things like crowd behaviour. Even sports teams will show very impressive coordination that is far faster than can be achieved by verbal guidance. Sure, this comes from having played together and learning specific configurations, but the teams learn optimal strategies to adapt to situations they encounter. The organism is no longer the individual players but rather the team."

"I suspect these organisms are themselves part of another higher level system operating at a scale that we haven't quite tapped into yet. They are like the cortical column in our brains."

"Whoa, if that is a column, the brain of this thing must be massive!" TechStaff exclaimed.

"It may not be physical size, Kim, but spatial scale. I don't think we have an appropriate reference for this, but these organisms may work across vast spatial scales that cover a much broader area."

"Not following." Sara frowned. "How does that translate to what we saw?"

Logan stepped forward. "I think I know where you are going with this, Ozzy. May I give it a try?"

"Sure." Espinoza raised his eyebrows to acknowledge.

"Let's think about a network like the Global AI." Logan brought up the schematic for its local configuration. "Here you see the nodes and, as our friend Terry can attest, if you factor in the variations in connections, you get an idea of the network structure, where certain nodes are important hubs for communication and others are peripheral."

"I still don't get it." Sara furrowed her brow.

"If we make these configurations more dynamic, like in our

brains, for instance, what is a hub at one point can become a peripheral node at another and then switch back to a hub. You can extend this across the entire network and visualize this reorganization at the level of the network." Logan looked at Terry. "Terry, if you would be so kind?"

Terry stepped forward and changed the display to show a video of network reconfigurations. The visuals showed portions of a network becoming more tightly linked while others were on the edge. Then the connections reconfigured to split the clusters.

"The thing about multiscale systems is that you may see this type of behaviour across spatial scales, within a local node or even sub-nodes," Logan continued.

Espinoza called out, "Brilliant, this is exactly where I was going. Let's suppose that this kind of reconfiguration happens with these organisms. We can actually see it at the scale that we are most familiar with, our bodies, but if these things are adaptive systems, it's likely happening below and above that scale."

"So, these organisms are part of a network?" Sara asked, feeling like she was comprehending. "But with no physical connections?"

"Yes, though, Sara, you know from our work together that physical connections don't need to exist," Espinoza added.

"Sure, depending on the scale. Cell to cell communication can be done by ionic flows triggered by protein release. I guess I am trying to make the link between the AI system and these Aliens, as we seem to be calling them now." Sara showed a flash of insight. "Oh wait, I get it. What we saw in the temple and sewer were nodes from a larger network. They may operate at the level that is the same scale as the AI system!"

"Or bigger," Espinoza added. "You have only been able to

monitor a small amount of their activity, but given the places they have operated, here and on the other side of the planet, they may have an even higher scale that is above the AI system."

"And then, there is the timescale issue," Katya added.

"Right. Each spatial scale will have a range of timescales they operate on. Smaller spatial scales have faster timescales, while bigger usually means longer. This means sometimes things happen on a fine scale that has no effect on a coarse scale. We call this timescale separation. But there are opportunities for one scale to influence another." Espinoza paused and looked at the rest of the group.

Logan said to himself, "If you know the rules that govern the evolution of behaviour across a manifold, you can estimate when flows on one manifold can influence flows on another manifold at a different scale."

Logan turned to Katya and Terry. "This could be it. This could be a perfectly executed example of a hierarchical complex adaptive system, wherein the space-time structures at each scale are causally linked."

There was silence in the room, mainly reflecting that no one quite understood Logan's insight.

"I love it when you talk dirty." Terry then stood. "If I get it, we could derive an algorithm that reveals this causal structure."

"Wait, I missed a step here," Sara said.

Katya tried to rephrase. "Logan has this idea of horizontal and vertical integration of complex systems. We usually deal only with horizontal, but the vital aspect, or maybe the secret sauce, is in how the scales affect one another. We've been working on this idea for years in the brain, but it's extremely difficult to get good data to test it. You need to measure someone every day for their entire life and do it for the entire population. I think what Logan has realized is that maybe these Aliens can give us these data."

"But this is more than an experiment," Sara replied. "They are messing with the AI system and maybe our climate. We have to do more than study their maths."

"Sorry, I didn't mean to suggest that," Katya offered. "Logan has the math in his head already. This is the opportunity for us to act on it."

"Yeah, fantasy becomes reality, eh?" Terry patted Logan on the back.

Logan laughed. "I will withhold my response to that comment, my friend." He turned. "Yvette, I know this will be a tremendous pain, but can you get us the data on the global climate system for the last year? If you can get it as the finest temporal resolution possible, that would be fantastic."

"I think so." She looked at her device, surprised by Logan's attention.

Logan noticed her reaction. "You are very familiar with these concepts, so I am confident you will know what sort of data we need."

Yvette smiled. "I understand."

Baren interjected. "I think we've done all we can here tonight. May I suggest we pack up and head back to our flats? We have an early flight tomorrow."

He turned to Xi, "Councillor Xi, I think we have what we need for now, and we will be in contact when we return to Headquarters.

Xi nodded, "Very well I think the BrainMaze interface you have provided to my engineers will keep them busy. I will make the preparations for your departure."

"Great. Thanks, Xi," Sara added. "Yvette, we can set up a link on the plane so you can grab the data en route. I am sure you'll find this more interesting than flipping through old Black Mirror episodes."

"Ozzy, thanks so much for helping us out." She turned to the video. "I promise to visit soon!"

"My pleasure, Sara. Please let me know your schedule. It would be great to host you and the rest of the team here. I'm sure there are all sorts of mischief we can get into." He laughed. "Safe travels."

The video feed ended.

As the team gathered their gear, Yvette stepped over to Logan. "Hey, thanks for pulling me in on this. I'm sorry if I was too harsh the other day. I feel a little vulnerable in this position, so maybe I get a bit too anxious."

"No problem, Yvette," Logan smiled. "We've known each other a while, so a few bumps here and there are expected."

"Thanks, Logan," she continued. "I'd like to see this one through. Do you mind if we work together on this number crunching on the plane? I am sure I can learn a lot here."

Sara's smartphone vibrated. She read the message from Doctor Shen on her device, "YOU'RE COLLEAGUE IS STABLE BUT WILL NEED A FEW MORE DAYS BEFORE I CAN RELEASE HIM."

"THANK YOU. WE HAD TO LEAVE BUT HE HAS THE MEANS TO GET BACK TO US WHEN HE IS READY," Sara replied. She would tell her team the news on the flight back to Berlin.

Chapter Four:
A catastrophe looms

A disastrous simulation

The data they compiled on the flight back was a gold mine for the simulations. When they landed, they went to the lab at the training facility, pushing the data into BrainMaze and examining the effects of the parameter specifications that were linked to the effect the Aliens had on the AI system.

"I am going to HQ and getting the briefing material ready for the next Council meeting." Sara got into her vehicle and looked over at Baren. "Sebastian, keep me posted on what you find."

Baren nodded as Sara drove away. He walked into the training facility and sat in the coffee room to review the messages on his device. He sent a note to Mitchell to say he would probably be home late that night.

In the lab, the results from another round of simulations using the new data were displayed.

"It's amazing how sophisticated the parameter choices are," Katya exclaimed. "With very subtle changes, they can start a cascade of huge effects that are way beyond what you would expect. They are masters of nonlinear systems."

"I think this comes from their ability to better appreciate the multiscale nature of complex systems in a way we are only beginning to grasp," Logan commented while watching another simulation. "You see how they manipulate changes on the fast time scale just prior to a bifurcation that completely alters how a slow variable evolves!"

"Sorry, what?" Terry glanced over at Logan.

"Usually, we think of slow processes as enabling changes in faster processes. For example, circadian rhythms, metabolism, weather seasons. Although it is rare, you could consider that a fast process may change in such a way as to shift the influence of a slow process so that the usual bifurcation does not happen."

"Or at least is less likely to happen," Katya added.

"Yes, of course," Logan acknowledged. "It biases the likelihood of an outcome, but there is still uncertainty."

Yvette continued to analyze the discrepancy between the predicted and actual weather patterns from the meteorological services. "It's hard to tell whether the examples of bad predictions are because of their intervention or the uncertainty in weather prediction."

Terry looked at Yvette's display. "Maybe we can focus on situations where the predictions on a shorter time scale were off. If I recall, most meteorological predictions are fairly accurate up to about 10 days, but beyond that, it gets hard."

"It's like a linear prediction model works for a 10-day horizon, but after ten days, the accumulated nonlinearities contribute more uncertainty," Yvette added.

"Yes, your idea's a good one, Yvette." Terry stared at Logan, who gave a nod of approval.

"Maybe we can start with events that were not predicted within a 10-day buffer and see if these show evidence of Alien intervention," Yvette suggested.

"That could work, but, careful, there is no easy way to know when a system is in a linear versus nonlinear regime. The prediction errors could reflect a nonlinear shift to a different regime rather than an intervention," Logan cautioned.

Yvette ran the analysis over the past five years. She noted an increasing trend for prediction errors closer to the present. Sunny days were predicted, but rains came. Quiet seas were predicted, but tropical depressions came. Snow was predicted, but the temperature was too high.

"One other thing that seems to be happening is that seasonal shifts are becoming more abrupt. Rather than a few weeks to glide from winter to spring, we see it happen in a few days." Yvette pointed to the seasonal graphs.

"It's like the entire system is becoming more nonlinear," she continued.

Logan rubbed his chin. "Or it could also be moving faster."

Yvette looked over at Logan. "Not sure I follow, Logan. We still get four seasons in most places."

Logan tried to clarify. "Well, we label them as four, but I am sure that the number of climate states is more than that. Early spring and late spring can be quite different, but we still call them spring."

"But when a system is close to a major bifurcation, the relative speed of the processes can change. The changes from snow to rain to sun are okay when spread across three months, but not when it happens in a week."

"Complex systems operate best at subcritical parts of their regime just before bifurcations, so what does pushing it across a bifurcation achieve?" Yvette asked.

"I can't be certain, but my guess is the Aliens are trying to enact a complete shift in the climate system. You can't do that by introducing a new attractor to the same manifold. You need to reconfigure the entire manifold, and this can only be done after a bifurcation."

Katya had been quiet, focusing her attention on the analytics that were coming out and trying to piece things together to get some coherence on the big picture.

"There is something missing for me in all this," she commented. "We have been focusing on relatively local events or at least continental. Can we look at the entire system?"

Yvette nodded. "You mean the entire planet?"

"Yes, exactly. The global climate is a closed system, so we should be able to see the effects of a volatile event in one hemisphere on the other hemisphere. Maybe this dependency is what's changed."

"Interesting idea, Katya." Logan smiled.

"I have learned a few things from you." She smiled back.

Yvette reran the analyses on a global scale.

"It's amazing to see it this way," Katya commented. "We focus on local events but forget that climate is linked across the planet."

They watched as the weather patterns in one hemisphere shifted with a change in orbital tilt. The gradual temperature gradient shift was punctuated by bursts, which represented storm systems. The global representation allowed for a better appreciation of the link between sea and sky as the temperature gradient across the oceans played out against the temperature gradients in the atmosphere.

"So, the climate system adapts to a fluctuation in one sector by shifting in another?" Yvette asked.

"I don't know that climate is an adaptive system in the way we usually consider CAS's. It is a complex *physical* system and shows interesting nonlinear features, but I don't think you can consider it adaptive," Logan replied.

"Well, certain species in the climate have had to adapt," Yvette replied.

"Yes, of course. Sometimes the labels are fuzzy, but physical systems do not have the same capacity for reorganization that adaptive systems do. This is why external influences on physical systems, like pollution, can have such drastic effects because there is no way for the physical system to adapt. They are nonlinear, but they do not adapt in the same way our immune system or brain does, for example."

Terry interrupted, "Hey, check this out." He pointed at the display.

"These north-south flows repeat, but look at the surrounding regions. They appear to be changing each time the flow happens, almost like it's setting up a new attractor."

"That's at the Pacific decadal oscillation, but its period has shortened," Yvette commented. "Or maybe the Interdecadal Pacific oscillation?"

"Or maybe a new one." Terry squinted.

The group watched the flow reappear, and the areas above the East Asian and west North American coast showed a redistribution of temperature gradients that persisted after the flow waned.

Logan stepped forward. "Let me try something." He entered a few commands and changed the display from a topographical map to a multi-dimensional manifold. The north-south flow occupied much of the manifold, but at each flow, the structure of the manifold shifted.

"Can we try to predict the outcome of a few more flows through that path?" Katya asked.

"I can do it using the parameter mappings we have. I hope we have enough data." Logan switched from analysis to simulation.

On the next two iterations, the flow continued to push the manifold structure so that small depressions began appearing at the extremes of the visible structure. On the next iteration, the valley of the main attractor deepened with strong temperature gradients forming all around it.

"That does not look good." Katya frowned.

"I think those are storm potentials," Logan replied.

"PROBABILITY MAPPING RECALIBRATING," was displayed.

"What's that mean?" Yvette asked.

"The manifold is changing, which means the probability that a certain area of the manifold will be visited is also changing," Logan replied, staring at the evolving trajectory.

The next trajectory proceeded. As it approached the main attractor, the edges of the basin collapsed, annihilating the attractor basin.

"It's like the closing of the Red Sea!" Terry exclaimed, thinking of scenes from the old movie *The Ten Commandments*.

"Literally, Terry. If the gradients reflect storm system potentials, their intersection will cause a massive temperature inversion over the Pacific Ocean." Logan grimaced.

Katya realized the implication. "That much of an energy shift would be disastrous! The storm's size would be huge, and obliterate the coastal communities!"

"I think it's clear that it's not *could*, but *would*," Logan added.

Terry interjected. "That assumes the probability mapping is accurate, though."

Logan looked at the bottom of the display to the certain functions.

"That is correct. The certainty here is not as high as I would like, but the probabilities are well above chance still."

The simulation continued. The manifold's collapse around the main attractor pulled the peripheral attractors to a more central location.

"Stop," Katya said. "Look at the edge down there. Where is that?"

Logan split the screen to show the new manifold coordinates on a flat map of the globe.

"The new attractors are very close to the locations where we identified the Alien hubs." She pointed to the Malaysian hub that they had just returned from. Another attractor was on the northwest coast in Canada.

"I don't understand." Yvette shook her head. "What are these new attractors?"

The simulation continued. New flow appeared that ran to one or the other of the new attractors, depending on the starting point.

Logan continued to watch the evolution. "It appears that the collapse is setting up a new series of paths. These are weather patterns, but given how integrated the Aliens are with our system, it could also be a new means of connecting their own hubs."

Katya spoke up. "So what we have is a collapse of our current climate system and a replacement by an Alien one."

"Yes, that would be accurate," Logan responded. "And the change will probably obliterate the current Pacific coast."

No one spoke for several moments.

Logan continued. "The new attractors could be entry points for the Aliens to exert further control. There is no doubt they have influence now, but if the collapse happens, I fear they will have complete control."

Yvette spun around. "We need to tell Sebastian and Sara!"

"Definitely, but let's do it in person. I have no faith that our communication systems are secure," Logan said as he ended the simulation. He extracted Terry's Motif and handed it back to him.

"Let's grab Sebastian, and we can go over to HQ and tell Sara." Yvette ran toward the door.

Terry's capture

Baren said nothing as he pondered the implications of the simulation. The rest of the group was silent as well. Baren turned to TechStaff.

"I would suggest we block communications at this point and get to Headquarters."

TechStaff looked to the trio for confirmation, but they were still scanning the simulation outcome for mistakes.

Terry spoke first. "I think Sebastian is right. I am not sure what communications are compromised anymore, so let's do what he suggests. I can put the simulation outcome on my Motif, and we can take it to Sara. It's risky, but I am certain she will want this to go to Council ASAP as too many lives are at stake."

With that, he downloaded the simulation results from BrainMaze. TechStaff prepared to activate the communication block but said, "Let me get the vehicle prepared for us from here, and I will start the comm block."

Baren nodded and moved to the door. Logan packed his gear, handed Katya her Motif and followed Baren. TechStaff looked up from her device as if to say, "Ready," and she followed Katya. Terry was the last to move, checking to make sure the simulation was still viable after the comm block. He examined the manifold and reoriented it to emphasize the Alien network and its links to the AI system. He caught himself marvelling too much at the elegance of the Alien network when he heard Katya call back to him, "Terry, we have to move now, please."

When they arrived outside, the bodyguards were standing next to the opened door on two vehicles. "There is always a chance that we have already been discovered, so we will take these two vehicles with one as a decoy. Yvette and I will ride with the BG's and stay with you until we get close and then take a parallel route to make sure we are not followed," TechStaff said.

The trio and Baren piled into the first vehicle and TechStaff, Yvette and the BG's in other. The vehicles moved as Baren spoke, "Phantom Mode." TechStaff had already programmed the destination and routing, so nothing more was necessary at this point.

"This is crazy," Katya blurted. "How can we even be sure that we can trust the Council with this? But if we do not proceed, I can't imagine the devastation that will occur." Her comment expressed what the others were thinking. "What if there is an Alien on the Council?"

"In open discussion, I am certain Sara can use the forum to avoid any overt blockage if there is an Alien on the Council or Aliens," Baren corrected himself. "The simulations are quite compelling, and the consequences of inaction will be seen as too embarrassing."

"Not to mention the genuine prospect of death," Logan added.

"Precisely," Baren concluded.

Terry was watching his Motif and seeing that simulations were still running. He saw one trajectory approach the Alien network and disappear. Terry rotated the manifold to trace this new trajectory, but could not. He went back to the original orientation and checked the parameter settings for that simulation. He then called up all simulations that showed a similar path, noting that most avoided this area, but a few showed a slight bend in its vicinity. Ghost attractor? Terry thought. Could it be?

He quickly focused a set of short simulations on the parameters that pushed the paths close to the area, ignoring conversation around him. Soon it was clear that the 'Ghost attractor' was indeed there, and any path with enough energy would enter the attractor, but there was no return path. *If we can push the Alien networks in this area, we could disconnect them from the AI system completely!* The thought flashed into Terry's mind.

"Hey, guys! I think I have an alternative solution!" Terry shouted.

His colleagues focused entirely on him.

"You remember the idea of ghost attractors that are remnants of a previous manifold, which can bias certain configurations for a system that are not obvious?" Terry spoke rapidly. "Well, I think I found one in the Alien's network configuration. We could use it to push them away from our system."

Terry's statement was interrupted by a sudden swerve in their vehicle. Baren looked to the sides and saw that they were surrounded by other vehicles that appeared to be empty.

"They found us!" Baren exclaimed as their vehicle swerved again to avoid a collision with their pursuers.

With the comm block, they could not contact TechStaff, but Baren saw the pursuers had effectively cut them off by surrounding them.

Logan said, "We should go into combat mode!"

"No, we are moving too fast, and there are too many civilians around." Baren countered and turned to the front of their vehicle, shouting, "Evasion mode!" Heavy-duty safety belts locked the occupants tightly into their seats.

For a few moments, their vehicle continued with no appreciable change. Then, almost imperceptibly, their vehicle slowed, which led to a gap in the formation of the pursuer vehicles. Their vehicle quickly moved into the gap and sped up ahead of the pursuers. Fortunately, the lane was clear, and they could put some distance between them and their pursuers.

Baren scanned for TechStaff's vehicle. He caught sight of them ahead.

"I think we will move to catch our colleagues," Baren said, just as two pursuers appeared on either side.

Their vehicle sped, quickly cut off one pursuer and took an exit off the main road. One pursuer followed, while the other continued along the main road.

"I don't see the other two," Logan said as he looked around. "Can we not track them?"

"With the comm block, it is difficult. The vehicle is not getting all the information it usually has to navigate, so it can only go on with the knowledge it has accumulated so far," Baren replied as he stared ahead.

"Perhaps we can link the vehicle with our Motifs to give it some extra computational power?" Katya suggested, trying to keep her gaze fixed ahead.

"Great idea, Katya!" Terry shouted, and he pulled out his goggles. "Let me try to sync up."

Baren glanced back uneasily. "I am not sure about that."

"Look, by adding another interface to the vehicle, we may find solutions the vehicle alone could not consider. Remember that the vehicle's repertoire shrinks when it's isolated from the system," Terry continued.

"Whoa," he said as he synced with the vehicle. On the display in his goggles, Terry saw the vehicle's small network focus on the immediate navigation and consider several options ahead.

It's so rare to see this real-time predictive modelling happening! Terry thought as the option space expanded to include the additional scenarios provided by his Motif.

"They are gaining on us!" Logan shouted, watching the pursuer closing in from behind.

Their vehicle made an abrupt turn back on to the main road. This brought them within a few metres of TechStaff's vehicle.

Logan smiled. "Nice."

The pursuer also returned to the main road, joining the other three that were rapidly closing in.

Terry watched the network dynamics testing different options. Their vehicle sped up to go in front of TechStaff. *A buffer,* he thought.

Their vehicle rapidly shifted over several lanes and exited the main street again, with TechStaff close behind.

Follow me, Terry thought.

The pursuers split up, with two following off the main road and two staying on it. The exit road ran parallel to the main artery road, giving entry and exit access for the community.

The team's vehicle did the manoeuvre several more times, moving between artery and feeder roads while randomly changing acceleration. This tactic kept an equivalent distance with the pursuers, as the uncertainty acted as a buffer.

"I think we will be getting close to our destination soon. If we don't lose them, we may need to move off and switch to combat mode. I don't want to take them any closer to Headquarters and risk exposure," Baren said with some urgency.

Their vehicle moved to a feeder once again, accelerating as it exited. This time a gap formed between their vehicle and TechStaff's sufficient for one pursuer to intervene. The collision-prevention algorithm in TechStaff's vehicle caused an immediate deceleration, putting even more distance between them.

As their vehicle moved to an exit, pursuers approached from the rear and side. The side pursuer nudged them, causing the team's vehicle to lurch into the guardrail on the exit ramp.

"Damn, damn, damn! Don't stop!" Logan yelled, but then he saw the other two pursuers had blocked the exit at the top.

Their vehicle screeched to a halt.

There was an eerie silence as the team looked around at the pursuers.

"PHANTOM MODE DISENGAGED" flashed on their vehicle's console.

"Baren, what are you doing?" shouted Katya.

Baren exclaimed, "It wasn't me!"

"TIME TO GO, PROFESSOR" now appeared on the vehicle's console.

Terry saw the Alien network connect with their vehicle.

An Alien materialized inside the vehicle between Terry and Katya. It touched Terry's Motif, and then the black and white skin engulfed him. Logan and Katya tried to intervene, but an energy blast repelled them.

The Alien disappeared and, along with it, Terry. His Motif and goggles fell to the vehicle floor.

Terry's Motif flashed: "SYSTEM ERROR."

On the way to appeal to the council

TechStaff's vehicle pulled up behind as Baren jumped out, signalling her.

"They've taken Terry. We've been compromised," he shouted as TechStaff opened the vehicle door.

"I don't understand. How did they take Terry when your vehicle was in Phantom Mode? No one can get inside." TechStaff checked her device to see if she could detect the Aliens' activity. Nothing was showing up on her screen. The pursuer's abandoned vehicles were on the roadway.

BGL ran up to the trio's vehicle. The vehicle's monitor was dark, as if the power was drained. "Hey, guys, are you okay?"

Logan sat up with a start. "Terry!" He reached the space where his friend once was.

Katya looked down at Terry's Motif. She was disoriented, but could see the "System Error" message flashing on the screen. She grabbed the device and sat back in her seat.

"Katya, are you alright?" Logan reached over to her.

"I am." She rubbed her eyes. "Give me a moment to link up to Terry's device."

The trio had biometric tags that linked to their Motifs and BrainMaze so that if they were separated from their devices, they could still be tracked. It is a system like "Find My Phone" but in reverse like "Find My Owner."

Katya entered her security information and reset Terry's Motif. As it reconnected to BrainMaze, the diagnostic program ran.

"BRAINMAZE LINK ESTABLISHED" it read.

"DATE AND TIME CONFIRMED."

"DATA LOGGING INTACT."

"CONNECTING TO PRIMARY USER."

"CONNECTING TO PRIMARY USER."

"CONNECTING TO PRIMARY USER."

"PRIMARY USER NOT FOUND."

"What?" Katya spoke softly.

By now, TechStaff had entered the vehicle. "Can you see him, Katya?"

"No, nothing. This is weird. The biometric tag is meant to connect us in any state, so even if we are injured or dead, the device should still be able to find us. It's as if Terry completely disappeared." Katya gazed up at TechStaff.

TechStaff had gotten used to Katya's confidence, but this was the first time Katya appeared uncertain.

"Maybe it's blocked, or the device is damaged?" TechStaff held her hand out. "I can take a look."

Katya handed it to TechStaff and sat back, trying to work through scenarios for why they couldn't track Terry. She startled when she realized that one scenario could be if they had completely annihilated Terry, destroying the biometric tag.

"Logan! What if they've killed him?"

She looked over at Logan, who was silently scanning outside the vehicle.

"Logan!" Katya tried to get his attention. "Did you hear me?"

Logan did not turn. "I think they came in through BrainMaze."

"What do you mean?"

"Exactly as I said. I think they came in through BrainMaze. In particular, it seems that they have somehow linked up with

Terry." He turned to Katya. "Consider that whenever he has encountered an Alien, it is when his Motif is connected, and the more intimate interactions are with him only."

"But what about the sewer? You were closer there."

"Yeah, but we chased it there. In other cases, they came to him. I can't be sure, Katya, but I think the Aliens may have hacked into Terry's biometrics directly."

"So, they hacked into Terry?" TechStaff said with her head slightly cocked.

"In a sense, I think so, yes." Logan rose to exit the vehicle. "Sebastian, we need to contact Sara as soon as possible. I think we are compromised more than we are aware."

He turned back to Katya. "I do not think they will kill him, Katya. They could have gotten rid of all of us easily. My guess is they've taken him and blocked the biometric chip."

The logic of Logan's assessment did not provide enough reassurance for Katya.

Baren was already speaking to Sara when he heard Logan's request. "Give me a moment, Logan," he replied. "Sara, we need to arrange an emergency meeting of the Council now and let them know everything. We've been working under the radar too long, and we do not have the resources to move further without the Council's blessing. We need the resources, and we need them now."

There was a pause in communication. Then came Sara's reply. "You're right, Sebastian. Get yourselves to HQ as quickly and as quietly as possible."

"Acknowledged." Baren turned to Logan. "Sorry, Logan, I was speaking with Sara. We are to go to HQ immediately. What were you saying?"

"You're one step ahead of me, Sebastian. I am going to ask that you contact her. I think the Aliens came in through Terry, so we might be more vulnerable than we think."

"I understand." Baren turned to BGK and BGL. "You two take Logan and Katya to HQ with TechStaff's vehicle. TechStaff and I will go with Yvette in the other vehicle."

BGL pocketed her smartphone. "I've called for a clean-up crew to get rid of the abandoned vehicles so we can get out."

"Well, we can't wait for them." Baren heard sirens growing louder.

"TechStaff, how strong is the frame in your vehicle?" Baren asked.

"It's seriously reinforced. I do a lot of off-roading, so we needed the extra strength," she replied.

"Can it clear the abandoned vehicles so that we may pass?"

TechStaff smiled. "Easily."

"Okay, then take your vehicle with the Professors and BGL, and I will go with the others. Hurry, please." The sound of more sirens filled the air.

TechStaff jumped into her vehicle. Katya and Logan were already there, and BGL followed. "Buckle up, please. This is going to be bumpy." TechStaff powered up her vehicle. "Manual Mode."

TechStaff backed her vehicle to the bottom of the ramp, pausing to make sure her path was clear. She slammed the control stick forward, spinning the wheels as they tried to grab the road.

Katya watched from the rear seat, surprised by the acceleration. She kept her eyes fixed on the abandoned vehicles. "Will we have enough momentum?"

"We'll find out in a sec!"

TechStaff's vehicle plowed into the intersection of the two abandoned vehicles, sending them spinning in opposite directions. Her vehicle showed only a slight reduction in speed.

"Whoa, that was very impressive!" Logan exclaimed, seeing Baren's vehicle following close behind.

"Phantom Mode," TechStaff yelled out just as they saw a parade of emergency vehicles approaching. She decelerated and pulled off to the side of the road, hoping that compliance with the rules of the road would take attention away from them. The emergency vehicles sped by, not noticing the slight damage to TechStaff's vehicle.

Appeal to the council

Baren led the group to the Council meeting hall, where Sara and a few Councillors were debating. The monitors in the walls were active, but only one had a live feed from Councillor Xi.

Sara was standing at the head of the table. "I know this breaks protocol, but this was the only way to get to the bottom of the mess with our AI system. You know how many levels of oversight there are to the AI system. It would have been impossible to get the information we have now without connecting the Professors directly into the entire global system."

Evans slammed his hand on the table. "That violates every principle we stand for here, Meyer! The entire purpose of the Council is to share information so that we can come to an intelligent consensus. You have completely ruined any credibility in that process."

DeValois followed Evans's comment. "What were you thinking, Sara? How can we ever have confidence in you again?"

Sara gathered herself. "The seriousness of the situation required rapid action, and I needed to be sure the information I had was legitimate. I realize I should have consulted with you all first, but consider the response if I had come to you with an accusation that the Council had been compromised with no tangible evidence? That's a political tactic used in dictatorial times to dissolve governments. I wanted to be sure about myself before I looped you in."

"I understand the rationale, but I cannot condone the action." Evans stared at Sara. "Does anyone outside the Council know what's going on?"

Sara shook her head. "We've been careful to keep it tight. The only ones are the Professors."

DeValois looked around the room at Baren and the others. "I see only two of the Professors. Where is the other?"

"This is why we are here now." Baren stepped to the table. "We have a formidable enemy at our gate who has taken the offensive and captured one of the Professors only moments ago."

"What!" Evans shouted. "Why are we hearing about this enemy only now?"

"We weren't sure until a few days ago." Baren looked at the monitor to Councillor Xi.

Sara sat down. "We were in Xi's jurisdiction and discovered the enemy activity. The Professors located them using the Global AI and their BrainMaze system. We had a few encounters with them and captured one. I can say for certain that this is an enemy you will not recognize."

"They are a life form that is some sort of merger of AI technology and biological networks. We don't know where they came from, but we do know that they have accessed our AI system and have been manipulating it to set some severe climate events in motion. The scale of these events is far beyond anything we've seen before."

The Council was silent for several moments.

"But when we last tested the AI system, it was fine. I doubt such a dramatic change would go undetected." DeValois expressed disbelief.

Logan was getting impatient. "Hey, look, they took our friend using no weapons. These beings are dangerous beyond our comprehension. They've been tracking us ever since we started working with you, and now that they have Terry, it may get even worse."

The Councillors looked at Logan with some surprise. "Please elaborate on your last comment to them, Logan," Sara spoke.

"Among the three of us, Terry probably has the best idea of the links between the AI system and BrainMaze. He knows the data better than any of us and also how to predict outcomes with great certainty. His statistical modelling expertise is unique, and if the Aliens get a hold of that, I am not sure we can counter effectively."

DeValois looked back at Sara. "Did he say 'Aliens'? Is that what you think they are? What kind of bullshit are you throwing at us?"

"If you don't believe me, ask Xi." Sara motioned to the video monitor. "Councillor Xi, can you please tell us what you saw in the examination room when we were there two days ago?"

Xi looked down and raised his head slowly. "There was a man who you shot when he tried to escape from you. Our medical team evaluated him and confirmed that he was killed by a bullet, probably from a Global Council weapon."

"What do you mean, a man?!" Logan shouted. "What the hell are you talking about?"

"The man you took to Doctor Shen. He is now dead, but we performed the autopsy to confirm what I just told you."

Logan was speechless.

"Xi, what the hell are you doing?" Sara tried to stay calm. "Do you not recall our video conference with Doctor Espinoza? What about the conversation about adaptive systems?"

Xi blinked. "Chair Meyer, with all respect, what I said are the events on the official record. There was no video conference that I can recall."

Sara felt a wave of anger. "I appreciate what's on record, Xi. What about what's off-record?"

Xi stared straight into his video camera. "My report stands as is."

TechStaff stepped forward. "Hey, we have the log of Terry's capture. We can show you that!"

"Yes! Do it." Sara motioned.

TechStaff connected her device to the display and tried to recover the preceding events from her log.

"I don't understand," she grumbled.

"What's wrong?" Sara turned to her.

"It's gone. The log's gone!" TechStaff stared at her screen. "Or maybe, it's been replaced."

She played the log. It began with the team entering two different vehicles and driving to the freeway. The vehicle with Baren and the Professors exited early. TechStaff's vehicle took the next exit and joined with Baren just outside the Council HQ. They parked the vehicles and entered HQ, at which point the log ended.

"That's not what happened!" TechStaff yelled. "Someone hijacked my log!"

"Someone, indeed." DeValois shook her head. "The log doesn't lie. You know it's almost impossible to alter the log. I don't understand what you are up to here, Sara, but this is not looking good."

Katya walked up to Sara. "Before we continue, can we please review the log again?"

"I don't see what purpose that serves..."

"Please, it will take only a moment."

DeValois sat back in her chair. TechStaff reran the log.

"Stop there." Katya walked up to the display. "Note two things here. First, Baren, Terry, Logan, Sara and I get into one vehicle, and Kim and the bodyguards get into the other. This is odd because you all know that Sara was here with you, not with us. Continue."

The log continued to the point where the vehicles stopped at HQ. "Stop here, please."

Katya pointed at their vehicle. "No Terry and no Sara."

There was silence in the room. Katya walked over next to Logan, who looked at her approvingly, mouthing, "Well done."

Evans was the first to speak. "What is your take on this, Baren?"

"It looks like the log has indeed been tampered with." Baren scratched his head. "We are in danger, and we need the Council's blessing to fight this."

Logan took that as a cue. "I want to add that the danger is more than just that the Aliens have infiltrated the AI system. They have set in motion a chain of events that will lead to a huge collision of storms over the ocean. We're looking at a convergence of storms that will set off a series of typhoons that will obliterate large parts of the Pacific Coast on both continents."

The room was silent again.

"How do you know this?" Xi spoke.

"We accessed the Alien system and conduct simulations that predicted the effects of their invention. The weather system collision is a certain outcome," Logan responded.

DeValois put her hands on the table and sat forward. "Are you certain of this?"

"Very. I can't give you the exact numbers at this moment, but we are in a situation where the cost of doing nothing would be tragic." Logan tried to stay calm. He felt the air of skepticism rising.

"What does your friend, Terry, think of this?" DeValois' sarcasm was palpable.

Logan clamped his jaw, breathed deep and spoke. "We did these simulations together as a team. When one member of our team speaks, they speak for the entire team."

DeValois gave a disingenuous smile. "I would like to believe that, but from what we've seen here so far, I don't trust you."

Evans looked over at DeValois with a furrowed brow. "I don't think we need to insult each other, Councillor DeValois."

"Apologies. I did not mean it as an insult. But considering what's on the table, there is nothing certain." She turned to Sara. "I can't condone what you are asking, Sara. There is not enough evidence for me to approve this support. And if the background story on how we got here ever got out, the Global Council would collapse."

Evans turned to Sara. "I am less skeptical, but we need more assurance before we can act. If you can bring concrete evidence,

I will support you."

"You've done too much damage already, Chair Meyer," Xi spoke firmly. "We cannot support you."

The opinions of the other Councillors at the table were divided. Small debates formed that revisited the arguments that Evans and DeValois made. None were as extreme as Xi, though there were a few sentiments that moved in that direction. Sara felt her control of the Council slipping.

"Please, please, everyone." Sara tried to get the proceedings in order. "Let me offer a resolution."

She stood up. "It's clear I have overstepped my office in taking the initiative I did, and for that, I apologize. As Chair and member of the Council, my obligation is to our citizens no matter where they are. I have the benefit of information that you do not yet have, and I am certain that if you had such information, you would have made the same decisions as I did.

"I propose we leave this matter as it is for now. The special operations team I have formed will continue to gather more tangible evidence and bring it back to the Council as soon as it is available. I don't think this will take much time, but I ask that you continue to trust me on this. You all know my history and that I would not act this way if I were unsure of the circumstances. This is why you elected me, Chair."

Xi cut his video feed abruptly. "I'll take that as an okay." Sara glanced at the table.

DeValois nodded. "It's reasonable, but for the love of God, please update us frequently. The last thing I need is someone outside the Council getting wind of this. Can you imagine what a field day our opponents would have if they heard that our Council Chair had gone rogue?"

Smiling, Sara said, "Of course. I am glad I can count on your support for this. I will make sure we move ahead together from now on."

"I hope so." DeValois was stern as she stood and walked away from the table. The other Council members were silent as they gathered themselves and also left.

Evans sat for a moment and looked at Sara and Baren. "Can I speak with you two in private?"

"Of course." Sara watched as the last Council member left. "Let's go to my office. It's secure, so no one will bother us."

She looked at Logan and Katya. "Why don't you head back to your hotel and get some rest? I will be in touch later."

"But we don't have time!" Logan protested.

"Logan, I appreciate the urgency and I know you're concerned for Terry, but we need time to recalibrate." Sara's voice showed both compassion and authority, "Please go with the bodyguards and I will contact you in a few hours."

BGK and BGL motioned to Katya and Logan towards the exit.

Sara walked across the room to a large wooden door that had a brass plaque with "Honourable Chair Sara H. Meyer" stamped on it. Sara always grinned slightly when she saw the plaque. If they only knew.

She opened the door and walked to a large table where she docked her smartphone. There was no desk in the office but rather tables of different sizes that accommodated anywhere from one to five people. There was a large sofa next to a massive window that looked over the city and a smaller one set perpendicular to it. Sara walked over and sat on the edge of the sofa.

"Please come and sit. This is my favourite place in the

building. I can't tell you how many times I've watched the sunrise and the sunset from here."

Baren walked over and sat at the opposite end of the sofa and Evans on the smaller sofa.

"Chair Meyer."

"Sara, please. We need not be formal in here, Joseph."

"Thanks." Evans was more subdued than usual, avoiding eye contact.

"Sara, I am anxious that there are members on the Council who do not have our best interests in mind." He rubbed his palms together.

He looked over at Baren. "I've mentioned this to you before, Sebastian. I've had some of my engineers look into the Global AI system. It seems there are, uh, Aliens, or something, that have infiltrated it, but they also saw activity that came from someone on the Council."

"On the Council?" Sara sat back.

"Yes. I can't be sure who, but sometimes we would implement a protocol from our deliberations that would get disabled when it was enacted. But it wasn't from the Aliens, Sara. It was from one of us."

Sara said nothing and continued to look out the window. The sun was approaching the western skyline.

Baren glanced over at Sara and back at Evans. "Have you discussed this with anyone else?"

"No, just the engineers and my deputy. We were going to bring it to you tomorrow, especially after the scene with Xi."

"You suspect Xi?"

"C'mon, Sebastian! You know that despite our best intentions to be civil, we harbour serious mistrust of each other. I had my people over in Xi's territory when you all were there. We couldn't tap into the conversation you had with Espinoza, but we saw the links that Xi made afterward. It's clear that he is not on our side. Here." Evans held up his smartphone and played back an audio recording.

"The recording only captured one side of the conversation." He set it on a coffee table.

Xi's voice was the first to come on. *"I have the creature bagged and will pass it on to you tomorrow."*

There was unintelligible noise with the occasional "must" or "vital" that came through.

"Yes, I know. I've sent your team the coordinates for the next AI connection so that you can put the block there. We have to try a different tactic this time. I fear that the BrainMaze system may have introduced a new fail-safe to avoid our usual approach."

The noise in the response was louder but no more intelligible. The word "eliminate" was clear.

"I understand. You can count on me. This next round with the Council will be the last. I am sure of it."

The transmission ended there.

Sara stared at Baren to gauge his reaction. Baren sat with his hands clenched in front of his jaw as if he had heard the worst news in the world. She turned to Evans.

"This is horrifying, Joseph, but," she sat up, "not surprising. I am, well, fuck it, I am pissed off that we didn't figure this out sooner, but now that we know at least one of the assholes that we need to deal with, it will make the next steps a little easier."

Evans laughed. "I am sorry I've never met this Sara before now! I completely agree. How do you think we should proceed?"

Baren leaned forward, smiling. "If you think this is

something, Joseph, you should see her after our annual meeting!"

"I think we are on the same page here. Perhaps the best thing I can do now is to analyze the communication more to see if we can decipher the other speaker. I will pass it on to Yvette and let Sara talk to Xi."

Sara stood up. "That sounds good. I think we are done for today. Joseph, could you please see yourself out?"

"Of course, Sara. I will be in touch when I get back to my flat." Evan stood, adjusted his jacket, and walked to the door.

As the door closed, Sara turned to Baren. "How long have you known that Xi was betraying us?"

"What do you mean?"

"I saw your reaction. It was far too contrived, Sebastian. We've known each other too long to play these games, and we're not kids anymore. I need," she paused and gathered her thoughts. "I should say 'we need' to be working from the same fucking playbook! Dammit, here we are at the peak of a crisis, and I find out that my team is actually playing for the other side, and my captain knew this?"

"Sara, please don't get so emotional." Baren stood in an uncertain stance.

Sara walked over to Baren. "How sad that after all this, the best you can come up with is 'don't get so emotional.' That's disappointing, Sebastian. I thought you were better than that."

Baren looked away, then back at Sara, shifting his jaw and trying to find the appropriate words. "It's been a tough couple of days, and perhaps I am not at my best. I think at this point, it's best if we call it a night and reconvene tomorrow."

"Agreed." Sara turned her back and walked to the window.

Baren left the office in silence.

Evans's ride home

Evans left HQ and waited in the driveway for his vehicle to arrive. He glanced at his device, saw no new notifications, and looked up to see his vehicle pull up to the gate. He pocketed his device and walked to the open vehicle door.

"Good evening, Councillor Evans. Where would you like to go tonight? We have received recommendations for some new restaurants that are on the way to your apartment."

Evans sat down heavily in the vehicle. "Food would be great. Just pick one, okay? Maybe something that's not too expensive, though."

"Of course, Councillor." The door closed, and the vehicle reversed away from the gate, turning onto the main road.

Evans began to reach for his device, but stopped. Enough for one day, he thought, directing his attention to the window, watching the cityscape evolve.

"We've been notified that there is an accident on our route to the restaurant and have been advised to take an alternate route."

"Fine," Evans responded as he continued to watch out the window.

The vehicle exited from the main roadway onto the smaller road along the river. The speed increased slightly as the traffic was much lighter. Evans looked out the other window to watch as the embankment grew taller, then back at the river. The water was flowing well, far more than would be expected given the hot, dry weather they had been experiencing. Evans was silently thankful for the efficacy of the AI system at water management for this sort of weather.

He looked forward and noticed the console flashed: "PHANTOM MODE."

"What's the problem?" Evans sat forward.

There was no response from the vehicle.

"Vehicle override!" Evans shouted.

The vehicle remained in Phantom Mode.

Evans pulled his device out and saw "NO CONNECTION" on the status window.

"Vehicle override, dammit!" he shouted again.

The vehicle sped up to an exit for a boat launch. The area was deserted; a few boats were tied to the dock. The vehicle drove on to the dock and sped up. As flew off the end of the dock, the doors of the vehicle opened. When it hit the water, the vehicle flipped on to its roof and sank as water rushed inside. Evans tried to unlock his seatbelt, but he was hanging upside down while the water poured around him. He held his breath and focused on the belt. He freed his arm but felt a sharp pain in his shoulder, suggesting that it was dislocated or broken. He refocused on the belt around his waist. The water had filled the interior, but air pockets in the chassis prevented it from sinking farther. The locking mechanism on the belt jammed. Evans tried to slide out from under the belt. His lungs were screaming for air, and his heart was pounding in his head. He gathered himself for one more effort, grasping the edge of the seat and pushing his hips back, sliding himself through.

He surfaced just ahead of the floating vehicle, gasping for air. He grabbed the edge of the vehicle, but his other arm was too numb to help. The river was calm, and the vehicle was almost stationary in the weak current. He caught his breath and looked around, hoping to see someone who could get help. He looked back at the dock to see a figure walking toward the edge.

"Hey!" Evans shouted, "Hey, help!"

The figure walked to the edge of the dock and glanced over at the vehicle. Evans saw the slight illumination from a device as the figure looked down and entered something, turned and walked away.

"Hey!!" Evans tried again, but stopped as he heard a distant rumble upstream.

"Ah, shit." He saw a giant rush of water approaching, which hit the vehicle, turning it over and submerging Evans. He lost his grip, blacking out as he sunk beneath the surface.

Alien integration

Xi's video feed went blank after the rush of water engulfed Evans. He clenched his teeth, knowing the overall situation may have just gotten worse.

A message came through. "EVANS'S SITUATION RESOLVED. WE HAVE PROCEEDED TO HIS OFFICE TO RETRIEVE THE RECORDS. ALL VIDEO RECORDS HAVE BEEN ERASED OR ALTERED."

"Acknowledged," Xi said.

"HAS THE ALIEN BEEN SHIPPED?"

"Yes. I have sent my chief scientist along, as well. She knows the Alien better than anyone and can also ensure my interests are addressed."

"THIS WAS NOT OUR AGREEMENT. I EXPLICITLY SAID THAT ONLY THE ALIEN WAS TO BE SENT HERE."

"THIS IS THE SECOND TIME YOU'VE DISOBEYED ME, XI. IF YOU CONTINUE THIS BEHAVIOUR, THERE IS A HIGH PROBABILITY THAT YOU WILL JOIN COUNCILLOR EVANS."

Xi was not a weak man. He had risen to power through a

calculated ruthlessness, and knew he had enough information to derail the initiative. His ruthlessness meant he had no hesitation acting aggressively, but was mindful enough to know to hold back to maintain an advantage.

"Your threats will not work with me. You forget that I have copies of all the documentation on the creature and some fascinating video footage. If I release even one of these, the entire plan will collapse. You should also know I have much less to lose than you do. No one will challenge me here. If we fail, I only lose a partner. But you will lose everything."

"VERY WELL. I WILL HAVE YOUR SCIENTIST WORK WITH OUR GROUP ON THE REANIMATION."

The communication ended. Xi checked his other communications feed and saw that his scientist and the Alien body were arriving at the airport in Berlin.

Doctor Ling, Xi's chief scientist, watched through her window on the airplane as the lights from the city emerged through the clouds. She hated flying, and in the small jet, the turbulence was worse than on large commercial airplanes. She could not relax or sleep, so spent most of the flight reviewing her notes from the study of the Alien and the videos of the first examination with Espinoza. She was convinced that something with an interface to biological entities helped to provide full animation of the Alien.

An announcement came over the speaker. "We'll be landing in one hour, Doctor Ling. If you want to freshen up, there is a bathroom with a shower in the rear. I believe there is also a fresh change of clothing in there."

They think of everything! Doctor Ling thought as she cautiously stepped to the door at the back. She opened the door, and there was a full bathroom with a dressing area and set of clothing that matched an outfit she had at home. She was impressed that they went to this trouble, but a bit uncomfortable that they knew so much about her fashion sense.

The plane landed as the sun was rising. It taxied for a while and came to a stop outside a hangar with "GC" emblazoned on the doors. The door of the plane opened. Doctor Ling walked forward, looking out to see a GC vehicle pulling up. The vehicle stopped, and its door opened.

"Welcome, Doctor Ling," the vehicle said as two people stepped out and moved to the cargo hold of the plane. "We will unload the cargo and leave for Headquarters momentarily. Please come in."

The cockpit door opened, showing a single empty seat and a large console. "I hope you enjoyed your flight, Doctor Ling," a voice said from the console. The plane had no human pilot.

She entered the vehicle. Once the cargo was loaded into the rear of the vehicle, the two attendants entered. "Global Headquarters. Phantom Mode," one of them said.

The trip to HQ lasted only 20 minutes, as it was early, and usual morning traffic had not started. Doctor Ling marvelled at the architecture and the combination of old and new buildings that naturally merged with one another. She had never been to Europe.

The vehicle approached the Global Headquarters, taking a turn to go around to the service entrance. The gates opened after the vehicle's ID was verified, and they proceeded to an open door entering the building.

Doctor Ling scanned the interior of the building, finding it hard to make out features in the dim light. The door opened, and the attendants exited, motioning for her to follow.

"Welcome, Doctor Ling," a voice called out in the darkness. "We are happy that you will be working with us." A person appeared in formal GC uniform.

"My name is Doctor Arias. I lead the science team here. I trust your flight was okay. Do you need anything?"

"Hello, Doctor Arias. I need nothing for the moment, thank you. How can I assist you?" Doctor Ling wasn't sure what she should say.

Yvette Arias smiled. "It's more how we can help each other. I have reviewed the videos and your work and am very excited to share some of my ideas. If you are feeling okay, perhaps we can get started right away?"

Yvette turned to the attendants. "Please take it to the lab in the back."

The attendants placed the black bag onto a gurney and wheeled it into the darkness.

"Follow me, please," Yvette motioned.

A door at the end of the room opened, sending a beam of light across the floor, acting almost as a beacon. Yvette and Doctor Ling entered.

The gurney sat next to a vat containing rust-coloured liquid. The room looked more like a repair shop than a lab, with an array of electronics and mixed tools on the walls.

"Sorry, this is a bit of a mess. Our main lab is being renovated, so we've had to make do with these temporary facilities," Yvette remarked as she closed the door.

"You haven't seen my lab." Doctor Ling smiled.

"Let's get started then." Yvette walked over to the gurney and opened the body bag. The Alien still maintained the humanoid shape.

"I want to move it into the vat. We've tried to recreate the liquid we saw them emerge from. I don't have the colour, but I think the basic elements are there." Yvette grabbed one end of the bag and motioned to Doctor Ling to help. Together, they picked the bag up and lowered it into the vat.

The bag and its contents slowly sunk in the liquid. The bag filled and sunk more rapidly, while the body floated midway in the fluid.

"We put in a small current pulse, similar to what Katya used in the video we saw. I think this gives the units some cohesion," Yvette said.

Doctor Ling smiled. "Very nice. I think this helps in the reanimation process. Our guess so far is that the organism can bind its elements through oscillations at matching frequencies. The noise bursts increase the ability to detect the weaker frequencies and enable synchrony across more elements."

"Sort of like stochastic resonance," Yvette suggested, "where weaker signals can be detected in the presence of noise but only in a nonlinear system."

"Yes, that is our belief. It may extend beyond the physical organism, which is why the fluid is especially important. It may carry the oscillations farther, allowing multiple organisms to interact at a distance.

"We think the organisms tune the noise to adapt to one pattern of frequencies, which is modulated to disengage and synchronize with another pattern. We haven't yet figured out what signals they change, however."

"I see," Yvette said. "But once they synchronize, they are effectively acting as a coherent entity."

"We believe so, though we haven't been able to test it."

"Then let's do it here." Yvette turned to a console and engaged the video display.

The display showed a top view of the vat with noise currents moving across in waves. The display registered small oscillations across the organism.

"I will send a 10-Hertz oscillation in the next noise wave."

As the wave passed, large sections of the Alien's body oscillated. Some sections merged and continued the oscillations. The sections desynchronized when the next noise wave came.

"I'll try a cluster of frequencies next."

This time, several small sections formed that oscillated at high frequencies. A low-frequency pattern was also present that connected the small sections.

Doctor Ling eyes widened. "This is perfect. The system is locally coherent at high frequencies and uses the higher power of the lower frequencies to link up the sections."

"And the noise bursts seem to enable the sections to disengage and reengage," Yvette added.

"This is essentially how many biological systems operate. Our brains do this through phases of coherent patterns and then desynchronize to form new ones. That shift between patterns is key to how we process information," Doctor Ling continued the line of thought.

"Our expectation was that if we could maintain such a pattern for the Alien, that could reanimate it. I think they contact one another through the liquid medium."

"We may be able to interface directly with the organism as it appears to be designed specifically to seek such coherent patterns." Doctor Ling stared at the vat.

She turned to Yvette. "I wasn't able to do this back at my lab, but I am certain we could synchronize it with one of us. The biological signals we generate spontaneously should be enough to reanimate it."

"I like where this is going." Yvette smiled as she walked over to the vat and handed Doctor Ling a data glove. "This takes pulsations from your arm muscles and transmits them. We use it for augmented reality simulations, but I think we can use it here to make the link. Would you like to do the honours?"

Doctor Ling hesitated for a moment and took the glove. "Since we isolated the organism from the rest of the system, I suppose it is safe."

"Agreed," Yvette said as she walked back to the console. "You'll need to immerse your hand in the vat. I will continue to send noise waves through the liquid, so you'll probably feel it."

Doctor Ling put the glove on and touched the surface of the liquid. There was no perceptible sensation.

She put more of her hand into it and noted some tingling at irregular intervals. "I feel them now," she reported.

"Okay, let's give it a few cycles and see if we get anything."

The display showed coherent patterns following the noise waves as before. This continued for several more seconds.

And then there was a shift.

The segments on the Alien's body close to Doctor Ling's hand started oscillating after each noise wave.

More segments engaged.

The coherent pattern spread across the Alien's body.

Then it moved.

"It's moving," Doctor Ling said. "I think I can feel…"

Her speech stopped when the Alien grabbed her hand. Immediately, segments engulfed her hand and then her arm. She watched as more segments ran up to her shoulder.

Her fear quickly turned to fascination, as she felt that somehow the segments were responding to her.

Stop, she thought, and the segments stopped.

Sit up, she thought, and the body rose from the vat.

She noticed she was seeing more than just what her eyes revealed. It was as if her brain were seeing with another set of eyes but looking at her. She saw an odd sort of digital version of herself, along with an image of Yvette and the console. Flows appeared that went between her, the organism, and the console. She was seeing the communication activities in the room.

Yvette sent a higher amplitude noise burst that disengaged the Alien from Doctor Ling. The segments slipped back into the vat as the body sunk into the liquid.

The abrupt noise burst disoriented Doctor Ling, who stumbled back and fell against Yvette.

"Whoa, are you okay?" Yvette tried to help her.

Doctor Ling felt a buzz in her head, but managed to stand. "Yes, I think so."

"This is fantastic!" she continued. "It was as if I could see both what I see and what it sees, like two feeds into my brain."

She felt her equilibrium returning and stood upright, removing the glove. "This may be a way to access their system. If we can see what they see but can control it, we may have the tool we need to communicate with them directly!"

Yvette smiled. "I think you are on to something. This could be exactly what we need.

"But first, I would like to get you some medical attention. I want to make sure the shock does not have any lasting harmful effects on you."

"I feel fine, Doctor Arias. Let's continue," Doctor Ling replied.

"No, it's best if we have you looked after." Yvette motioned to the attendants, who approached Doctor Ling.

"I am fine, really. This is unnecessary!" Doctor Ling insisted.

One attendant grabbed Doctor Ling's arm, while the other injected a tranquilizer.

As Doctor Ling lost consciousness, she heard Yvette say, "Don't worry. We will tell Xi and your family you've had an accident, but you are in medical care."

She turned back to the console and sent a message to Baren. "HAVE MECHANISM TO ENTER ALIEN SYSTEM. I WILL MEET YOU IN THE COMMUNICATIONS HUB."

Chapter Five:
Logan's Run

Logan in the stairs

The Global Council vehicle dropped Logan, Katya and the bodyguards at the apartment-hotel.

"Let's talk in my flat," Katya whispered to Logan as they entered the lobby and walked to the elevator.

"We're going to do a perimeter check and will be up in a moment," BGL called to them.

Logan started ranting as they entered. "The Global Council has no clue! They're completely blind to the threat. Their ignorance of the Alien intrusion was appalling. It's like they chose to ignore it, rather than take responsibility and risk embarrassment.

"And Sara wasn't much better. She was hopelessly conflicted in her role as the Council Chair and as the de facto leader of the Special Ops teams, but now she suffers from the same decision paralysis that she criticizes! We need more resources than just this little makeshift team."

What frustrated him the most was the complete ineptitude of the Special Ops team in trying to prevent Terry's abduction. "And nothing from our supposed bodyguards. Do they expect a scientist to battle these things?" His voice grew louder. "By now, they are probably sucking his brains out to get access to BrainMaze!" He had no idea if what he was saying was true.

Katya walked over to touch his shoulder. "We have to believe he is okay, Logan. There is no benefit in imagining the worst. Besides, we have seen no evidence that the Aliens are aggressive in that way."

"No evidence? I'd say chasing us down a highway and snatching Terry counts as aggression! I don't understand you sometimes, Katya. We need to get Terry back!"

"Logan, stop and think for a moment. How will we do that? With our communications hubs compromised, we cannot trust any data at the moment. There is nothing more we can do until we hear from Sara or Sebastian, and I feel they will be arguing with the Council members for a little while longer."

Logan took a deep breath. "I know, Katya, but I feel helpless now. It's like there is nothing we can do, and when we try, we are blocked."

He pivoted toward Katya. "I need to clear my head. I need to go for a quick run."

"I will go with you." Katya turned to grab her goggles and running gear.

"Let me go alone, Katya. I need the time to think," he asked.

Katya sighed. "As you wish. Please take your Motif and goggles in case we need to connect. And take BGL with you."

Logan nodded and left to go to his room. BGL was waiting in the hallway.

"I need to go for a run. Would you like to join me?" Logan said with an unintended growl.

"Of course," BGL replied. "I can run in this outfit, so I will wait for you here."

"Fine," Logan went to his room. He changed his shoes and realized that his uniform would be too good for running. He placed his Motif in his back pocket, took his weapon out, placed it on the desk, and put on the goggles. "SYNCED" it showed.

Logan left his room to see BGL doing some light stretches. "I am a bit tight," BGL said as she rotated her torso.

"Let's go," Logan said, and hurried to the stairwell. He ran down the stairs with BGL close behind. When they exited the building, Logan paused and turned to BGL.

"I am sorry if I seem a little, uh, curt, is it?" Logan apologized. "Katya and I disagree on the situation, so I need to get out to blow off a bit of steam."

BGL nodded. "I will let you run in peace. I'll stay a few paces behind you." She put her goggles on.

"Thank you," Logan said. He took the reverse route they did along the river the other day, staying on the smaller roads but avoiding the river trails. He brought up the map on his goggles and confirmed that BGL was behind him.

Logan increased his pace a little to clear his head. He couldn't get the image of the Alien entering and disappearing from the vehicle after engulfing Terry out of his mind.

His pace picked up as he approached the first bridge over the river.

If these are elemental beings, they must be able to reduce themselves to a small enough dimension to pass through our security systems. He thought this explained how the Alien materialized in their vehicle.

I cannot understand how they took Terry unless they can act on biological tissue. He crossed the bridge and turned to go down to the path along the river. The lights along the path were flickering, giving the sense that something was amiss in the power system.

Logan glanced at the path and noted that BGL was about 25 metres behind him. *She keeps a consistent pace.*

He concentrated on his cadence to clear his thoughts.

If these creatures can interact with biological tissue, what's to stop them from taking over a body?

The thought focused his attention.

If this is possible, perhaps some of the Council have already been taken over!

The path shifted closer to the river. Logan could see the suspension bridge ahead, where they avoided the flash flood only a few days ago. He was now certain the Aliens caused the flood.

I am seeing how this works. They probably figured out we discovered how they accessed the Global AI system and wanted to eliminate us before we could alert the Council.

They must have hacked into BrainMaze early on.

The idea infuriated Logan. They had spent countless hours on the security of BrainMaze, using principles of adaptive systems to detect any non-adaptive activity and eliminate it quickly. That the Aliens circumvented their security angered and worried him.

I don't know how we will find Terry if they are accessing BrainMaze too!

Logan ran harder now, eager to get back to the hotel and talk with Katya about his suspicions. He glanced at the map again, smiling as he saw BGL was keeping pace with him.

His foot hit the first plank on the suspension bridge, sending a wave across that was far more intense than he remembered when they crossed it before.

The flood must have damaged it. Logan slowed his progress to steady the bridge. He felt the vibrations when BGL stepped on the bridge and turned to caution her.

A surge of water approached them but, this time, not high

enough to put them in danger. Logan stopped to watch the water stream past.

An overturned vehicle passed beneath them.

Logan looked back at BGL, who was watching the vehicle.

"That's a Global Council vehicle," she called out to him. "We'd better get back to the hotel, Logan. This does not look good."

"Okay," Logan called back and proceeded slowly along the bridge, glancing down to see the water surge dissipate. BGL paused on the bridge to communicate her observations and followed Logan.

Once his foot hit firm ground, Logan turned and picked up the pace along the river path. He avoided the forest, staying closer to the more visible path for safety and to cut down the time to get to the hotel.

When they approached the hotel, BGL called out. "Hey, I'm going to do a perimeter check again and meet you at your room. Do you want anything from the cafe?"

"No, I think I will be okay," Logan shouted. He watched BGL jog around the side of the building, and he walked up the drive toward the entrance, stretching his leg using a concrete barrier for support.

A warning signal flashed on Logan's goggles.

He waited for more information and activated his B2S feed.

BGL sent a message, "LOGAN, POSSIBLE ALIEN HEADING YOUR WAY."

He saw what appeared to be an Alien running from the entrance. Although the Alien's face was obscured by a hood, Logan could see the white hands.

Katya! he thought. *Are you okay?*

"YES, WHAT'S UP?" he saw.

I just got a warning signal and saw an Alien outside. I am going to pursue, he thought as he ran after the Alien.

"WAIT, LOGAN. WHO SENT THE WARNING? IS BGL WITH YOU?"

He ignored Katya's question and continued the chase.

The Alien ran across the main street between traffic signals to avoid the vehicles. Logan sprinted after, but stopped when a vehicle nearly hit him in the intersection. The Alien seemed to know Logan was in pursuit and cut across another road. Logan had trouble navigating as several autonomous vehicles swerved to avoid the Alien and hadn't course-corrected before they needed to do the same for Logan. *Clever!* Logan thought.

The Alien increased speed now on the sidewalk, weaving around pedestrians and other obstacles. The hood obscured the facial features enough so that the people on the street didn't notice.

Logan was closing in on the Alien.

"LOGAN, WE ARE TRACKING YOU AND ARE COMING YOUR WAY."

The Alien quickly turned into a building. Logan nearly missed the turn, grabbing the door handle to shift his momentum. He saw the Alien enter the stairwell and descend. Logan ran to the top of the stairs but stopped to see that the stairs going down were dark. He scanned for a light switch and pressed it.

Nothing happened. The stairs remained dark. Logan tried again, switching off and then on, with no effect. His mind quickly pulled up a statement from Terry. *You know you are in a dream if the lights don't work. Just like in the movie Waking Life.*

Logan thought for a moment and felt confident he was awake, but was uncertain how to proceed. *I left my damn weapon in the room!* He remembered.

He looked around for something that could act as a weapon. To his left was a utility closet that was unlocked. He opened it and saw several metal pipes that were probably remnants of old plumbing. *This may help,* he thought as he grabbed one pipe and turned back to the stairs.

Logan scanned his display and reset the goggles to Night Mode. The lens changed, giving the stairs a dull orange hue. Logan looked as far down the stairs as he could see, but the stairwell turned near the bottom. He climbed down the first flight and looked down again. He could make out the bottom of the stairs, but could not see the Alien.

"LOGAN. WE ARE ALMOST THERE."

He continued down. He saw movement on the last set of stairs and ran down after it.

"I don't want to hurt you!" he called out. "I only want my friend back. Please, let's just talk this through."

As Logan arrived at the bottom of the stairs, he saw the Alien standing in front of him, with its back to him. It seemed to be looking at something ahead, but Logan could not see around it.

Logan tapped the pipe on the floor. "C'mon, we aren't going anywhere, and I am not in the mood for a fight. Let us talk, okay?"

The Alien raised its hand as if to ask Logan for silence. A wooden door opened in front of the Alien, and a faint light emerged. Logan still could not see around the Alien, so he moved forward slowly.

"Hey, really, I just want to talk." The Alien turned its head to look at Logan.

The face was that of a child, but with piercing eyes that froze Logan in his steps. The Alien turned its body to face Logan, which gave Logan a moment to see the large shape that occupied the doorway.

The child's face melted in front of him, replaced by a featureless black and white facade. The white pieces moved at random, with the black patches remaining still. The Alien reached out to Logan, but Logan backed away.

"You are not touching me! I was there when you took Terry! I will crack your skull before I let you do that to me!" Logan held the pipe like a baseball bat.

The Alien stepped toward Logan, reaching. Logan swung the pipe around, hitting the outstretched hand. It shattered like glass, scattering black and white fragments.

The Alien did not flinch, calmly stepped back and turned, walking toward the door. As it entered, the shape that had been in the doorway came into view. It seemed like a massive dog or cat at first, moving like a cat, but with the bulk of a large dog. Its grotesque head came into view. Logan positioned himself for an attack.

The creature's face looked like no animal Logan had ever seen. Its snout was that of a large canine, but its eyes were human. There were no visible ears on its head. The eyes stared at Logan, almost as if to judge him. The creature made a low growl and opened its mouth. The mouth appeared to grow larger. Or was the creature coming closer? Logan could not tell.

A low moan emerged from the creature. "You are trapped, Logan. You are with us now." Logan thought he heard, but did not know the source. He felt there was only one choice left — to fight.

"Fuck you!" Logan screamed as he jammed the pipe into the creature's mouth. In that moment, Logan's world exploded in a bright light that filled the stairway to the main floor.

When the light faded, the door was closed. The pipe and goggles lay on the ground. Logan was gone.

Katya's obstacle course

"ALIEN ENCOUNTERED OUTSIDE. I AM GOING TO PURSUE," Katya read on her Motif. She immediately put on her goggles to sync up.

Wait, Logan. Is BGL with you? she thought, knowing that Logan had already gone.

She alerted BGK, Baren and TechStaff. *Logan is in pursuit of a possible Alien. I do not know if BGL is with him. Meet in the lobby immediately so that we can help him.*

Katya put on her jacket and hat and grabbed her weapon. She checked the display in her goggles to see if anything more was coming from Logan. Although his position was being relayed, his camera feed was not, which gave her a greater sense of urgency.

She ran down the stairs into the lobby, finding BGK and TechStaff waiting for her. "You are quick!" Katya exclaimed.

BGK said, "Kim alerted me just before you contacted us. She'd been tracking Logan and saw that he took off on his own without BGL."

TechStaff peered at Katya. "Sorry if it sounds intrusive, but since we just lost Terry, I thought it'd be a good idea to track you guys whenever we can't see you."

"No need for apologies. I am pleased you took the initiative." She scanned the lobby. "Where is Sebastian?"

"He is at Headquarters, meeting with Sara and a few Council

members. He said he would contact us later," BGK replied.

"Okay, we should go now," Katya said as she moved to the hotel entrance. "Logan is still in pursuit, and it looks like they're about a kilometre away."

As they approached the door, the Bell Captain commented, "Out for another evening run, Professor? It's a good night for it!"

"For sure!" Katya replied as she put on her goggles and sprinted outside.

Once they got to the road, they paused briefly. "Do we know where BGL is now?"

TechStaff checked her feed. "Not at the moment. She is not registering in my coverage. Shall I see if she went back to Headquarters?"

"No, let's go," Katya said and began running again.

Katya felt the urge to sprint, but not to get too far ahead of TechStaff and BGK. Her display indicated Logan was also still running, which gave her some relief that there was not yet a battle.

"Down here!" she called out as they turned down the street of Logan's latest path.

"Stop!" TechStaff yelled after they ran about 400 metres. "I think he's inside a building around here." Katya checked her display, confirming that Logan had stopped. His signal was unsteady, making his position uncertain.

"Where are all the people?" BGK looked around. The street was deserted, save for a few feral cats.

"This is an old industrial neighbourhood that is being rebuilt. Most of the buildings are under renovation or scheduled for demolition, so they are empty." Katya pointed down an alley between the buildings. "The river is just down there where the old port was."

TechStaff tried to get a better fix on Logan's position. "He must be in a basement or something, but I can't tell which building."

BGK said, "He's got to be in one of these. I will check this one. Katya, check that one, and TechStaff, that one." BGK gestured. "Stay in constant contact, and if you see something, do not engage until I am with you." BGK disappeared into a doorway. Katya and TechStaff moved to the other buildings.

An enormous bright flash shot out from the building BGK just entered.

"He's in there!" Katya yelled as she moved with TechStaff closely behind.

The building was eerily quiet when they entered, as though all the sound was absorbed. Their steps seemed muffled. TechStaff tapped Katya's shoulder and showed her the tracking signal on her device. She pointed to suggest that Logan was in the stairwell. Katya acknowledged, but scanned the area to see where BGK had gone. She signed the letters "BGK" to TechStaff, who shrugged her shoulders.

The two walked to the stairwell, noticing the door to the utility closet was open. They checked inside and saw nothing other than a pile of pipes. Katya took her weapon out and began a careful walk down the stairs. TechStaff glanced over the rail and followed.

They continued going down until they came to the base of the stairs, where they faced an old door that was chain locked. On the ground, they saw another pipe and a pair of goggles. *Logan*, Katya thought.

TechStaff examined the area. "Katya, I don't think there is anyone else here. I don't know how BGK got out unless through this door." She looked at the goggles on the ground. "Are those Logan's?"

Katya picked up the goggles and examined them. Seeing the numbers on the frame, she said, "Yes, they are."

"Excellent!" TechStaff exclaimed. "I can patch in to see if we can get anything from them to see what may have happened."

"You can do this?" TechStaff's skills surprised Katya once again.

"Yes, we worked out an interface that allows us to check the goggle's memory," TechStaff said as she reached for the goggles from Katya. The goggles had a small memory buffer that kept the last several minutes of what the user saw to help with the video record in case there was an interruption from the signal.

TechStaff scanned the number on the goggle frame and turned to Katya. "I need your authentication to access this. We set it up so that only the three of you have access."

"I appreciate that," Katya said and gave her authentication.

TechStaff projected the video feed into the air. The image was grainy and had several sync errors.

Video began with what looked like shattering black and white glass, followed by a figure walking to the opened door. An animal of some sort appeared in the image, moving toward the viewer. It flickered several times as its head moved in focus. The head filled a large part of the image and then its mouth opening. There was a muffled yell and a bright flash. The video looped back to the door.

"What the?" Katya exclaimed as the video looped again. "Is this accurate? I have never seen such a creature before. Is it an Alien?"

TechStaff paused the video. "I can't say for sure, but there are problems. Look at the door in the video and then at the door over there." She gestured. "The one in video is wood, while the one over there is heavy steel. Also, the size is all wrong. If the door in video were here, it would be at least another half metre wider."

"So, is this a false memory?" Katya clenched her teeth.

"Uh, I think it's worse than that." TechStaff paused and checked the diagnostics. "Damn, someone hacked Logan's goggles!"

"How is that possible? No one has access to these other than the three of us. You just said that the authentication protocol prevents this." Katya grew angry.

"I don't know yet. But someone definitely hacked these. Look, when the Night Mode was activated, there was something else being fed into Logan's goggles. He may have thought what he was seeing was real, but actually, it was a virtual reality feed like the ones we used for training."

"Okay." Katya collected her thoughts. "The flash we saw outside is probably the same flash in the video based on the timestamp. We got down here quickly, so I don't know how whoever did this would have gotten out unless they went through that door. But the door is chained from this side." Katya walked up to the door and examined the surrounding area.

"Look, it's been opened recently. The dust is pushed away from the door sweep and look here — there are marks on the chain as if someone just handled it," Katya pointed.

"But who would have locked the door..." TechStaff's eyes widened. "BGK?"

Katya grimaced. "Yes, I believe so. I have not trusted these so-called bodyguards since I met them. They seem too cavalier and ineffective."

"But where is BGK now? He would have passed us on the stairs," TechStaff wondered as she looked up the stairs.

"At this point, I don't care. If Logan is still alive, they took him through this door, and we need to follow," Katya snarled.

"But it's locked…" TechStaff barely finished before Katya used her weapon to blast the lock on the chain.

Katya pulled the door open to reveal a corridor that vanished in the distance.

"I do not believe it would be wise for us to use the goggles at this point," Katya commented as she scanned the corridor. "Do you happen to have…"

TechStaff smiled. "Light 'em up." She pulled two flashlights from her hip pack, handing one to Katya. "Excellent!" Katya said, taking the light and affixing it to the top of her weapon.

"Katya," TechStaff whispered, "before we go in there, we probably should let someone know."

Katya paused. "You are right, of course. I would say the same thing if I were you."

"Send a message to Sara and Sebastian, but do it through BrainMaze connections rather than the AI system. Let them know we are in pursuit of the Aliens who may have just abducted Logan." Katya turned to look down the corridor, cautiously shining the light ahead as TechStaff composed the message.

"Done," TechStaff reported. "We can go now."

The pair walked into the corridor, staying close to the walls as they proceeded. Cobwebs lined the walls of the corridor, but the dust on the floor was recently disturbed. Katya pointed to the marks along the floor, suggesting something was dragged recently, likely Logan.

As they continued, the marks disappeared. They backtracked

to see if they had missed an exit. Katya signalled that they picked Logan up to carry him, and they should move ahead.

This was confirmed 40 metres when they came to a junction of two corridors. There was Logan's Motif on the ground. TechStaff picked it up and handed it to Katya, who saw the device had gone into "StandBy Mode," having been disconnected from its primary user. The signal was too weak to get a reliable fix on Logan's biometric tag.

TechStaff considered both corridors. "Should we each take one path?" she signed to Katya.

"No, we need to stay together," Katya signed back.

They peered down both corridors and saw the left one had a stairwell visible, while the right seemed to continue for some distance. Katya motioned to move down the left corridor and ran ahead, followed by TechStaff. They reached the stairwell and glanced up. As Katya's light reflected off the stairs, they heard a door open and slam.

"Let's move!" Katya shouted and ran up the stairs. The pair came to the door at the top and paused. TechStaff pushed it open slowly, and Katya extended a small mirror out the door. She saw someone running away and burst out the door.

The runner appeared to be an Alien, judging by the white arms, but was facing away from them as it dashed down the alley.

Katya and TechStaff pursued. The Alien hit the street in full stride and crossed into the next alley. The pair paused briefly and crossed the empty street into the alley. They tried to catch up, but the Alien maintained the pace.

It came to a fence that paralleled the alley and jumped. Katya did not break stride and cleared the fence. TechStaff struggled momentarily at the top of the fence but cleared and caught up to Katya. On the other side was a long field that seemed to lead to the river.

"We can't let it get to the river!" TechStaff yelled out.

Katya stopped and dropped to one knee, aiming at the Alien. She tried to aim low and pulled the trigger.

The projectile impacted just behind the Alien.

She fired again. The Alien made a quick turn, and the projectile hit where its leg would have been.

The Alien turned quickly down another alley.

"Go!" Katya shouted, and the pair resumed their chase.

"That's a dead-end!" TechStaff shouted as they ran. They came to the alley entrance to see the Alien scaling the drainpipe that ran along the side of the building. Katya ran in and climbed as well. TechStaff sighed. "This is what I get for skipping the obstacle course training."

The Alien jumped through an open window three levels up, closely followed by Katya. As Katya jumped in the window, the Alien surprised her and knocked her down, sending her Motif and weapon sliding across the old wooden floor. Katya quickly rolled onto her back to assume a defensive posture and saw that the Alien's face was black and featureless. It was breathing heavily and made a posture as if it was going to attack. Just then, TechStaff came to the window and yelled, "Stop, I have you in my sights!"

The Alien ran out of the room. Katya sprung up and grabbed her weapon and Motif. "I should have remembered the training!" She ran to the door, with TechStaff close behind.

Entering the hallway, they saw the Alien going up the stairwell. Katya kept her weapon out, vowing to use it at next chance. However, the stairs were narrow, making it difficult to get a clear view of the target. They continued to climb, hearing the Alien exit through the door at the top of the stairs.

At the top, Katya paused and gently opened the door marked "ROOF ACCESS ONLY," extending a mirror to see if it was clear. The Alien smashed it and then ran to the edge of the roof. Katya raised her weapon but could not fire before the Alien leaped off the edge.

"Damn you!" she screamed and ran to the edge to see the Alien had landed on the roof of the next building. Katya holstered her weapon and ran back toward the door and then turned in full sprint.

TechStaff watched as Katya sprinted to the edge. "Katya, stop!" she yelled too late as Katya leaped from the edge of the building toward the other roof below.

TechStaff heard a thump as she ran to the edge.

Katya had almost made the jump, falling just short but clinging to the edge of the roof. TechStaff gasped, looking for a way to help. She looked across to see the Alien approaching where Katya was hanging. "Katya, look out!"

Katya struggled to find some footing, jamming her toes on her left foot around the brick. Her right foot found no purchase but steadied her balance. Her hands were firmly gripping the edge, and she began to climb. She looked up to see the Alien's black visage.

"No net to save you this time, eh, Professor?" the Alien said, reaching for her hand.

Katya heard a weapon fire and saw the Alien fall back. She looked back to see TechStaff with her weapon pointed toward them.

Katya scrambled up the wall and onto the roof.

The Alien was gone.

"Katya! Are you alright?" TechStaff yelled.

Katya thought her ribs might be bruised. "I think so, yes. Good shot! Did you hit it?"

"Thanks. I think maybe in the shoulder or chest. Is it there?" TechStaff asked.

Katya shook her head, "No."

"You stay there, okay? I will come over." TechStaff signalled as she turned to walk back to the roof entrance.

"I am okay. I will meet you on the street in a moment once I catch my breath." Katya sat back on the edge.

Katya felt her pulse slowing and her breathing steady, then realized something was not right.

The Aliens we saw in the sewers and the one who took Terry did not need to run. They seemed to come and go without effort. Why did this one run? She wondered as she walked to the other side of the roof.

She looked around at the other buildings to see any sign of her opponent. A flash of light from an open door on the street caught her attention. Katya moved closer to the edge and peered down at the building. There were windows in the stairwell, and she thought she saw someone climbing them. She reached into her pocket to pull out a small set of binoculars and scanned the stairwell. It was definitely the Alien. The hood no longer covered its head, and there was some white peeking out of its neck where the black from the face ended. She lost sight of it.

She scanned the windows along the floor where she had last seen the Alien. Another flash of light suggested someone entering a room. She fixed her gaze on that window and waited.

The light in the room was dim, but she could make out the

Alien as it entered the room. As it paced, it removed its hooded jacket to reveal a bullet-proof vest, rubbing the place where TechStaff's projectile likely hit.

This is odd, Katya thought. *Why would it need a flak jacket?*

The light levels in the room changed again, suggesting another entrant. As she watched the person approach the window, it was very clear who it was. "BGK! So there you are!", she said under her breath.

BGK walked back away from the window, looking toward the Alien. An unconscious Logan lay on a sofa behind BGK. The Alien lifted its hand up, grabbing the top of its head and pulling it up, removing the black as if it were a piece of cloth.

Or a mask, Katya thought. As she continued to watch, she grew increasingly angry at the betrayal of BGK. *Who is your bastard friend?* she wondered as she watched the Alien move toward the window.

The Alien turned to look out, allowing the dim light to illuminate his face.

"Baren!" Katya gasped. "Sebastian!"

She moved away from the edge of the roof. *We are seriously messed up*; she thought.

Katya found the door on the roof and quickly descended. She came out from the side entrance at street level and searched for TechStaff, who was standing close to the side of the building.

"It was Baren!" Katya said through angry teeth. "It was him in the Alien outfit. BGK seems to be in on it too."

TechStaff looked at Katya for a few moments as she considered her next words. "I am so sorry, Katya. I think Sara was getting concerned about him, and I had my own doubts honestly."

"So now we have two enemies, it seems," Katya said, looking up at the building where she'd seen Baren and BGK.

"Katya, I don't think there is anything more we can do now. I've called a vehicle, and it should be around the corner, out of sight of our 'friends' upstairs. Let me take you home, and I will talk to Sara to see what we should do next."

Katya felt the pain in her side increasing a little. She groaned a little. "I like that idea. I think I am done running for now."

Chapter Six:
Terry's release

A debate with a Londoner

The green walls around Terry showed another slight shift in hue.

"Did you want something to eat?" he heard.

Terry stood up and looked around. "What?"

"I said, did'ya want somethin' to eat?" A white and black humanoid materialized. It was featureless on details like fingers, toes and face. It spoke with a heavy British accent.

Terry stepped back. "Are you able to read my thoughts?"

"Nah, figured that since you've been here a while, you might be gettin' a bit peckish," it said.

Terry grimaced a bit. "Are you talking now? Since when do you speak with a British accent?"

"I dunno, you Canadians tend to like the British accent, so we figured you'd feel more comfortable."

Terry suppressed a laugh. "Uh, sure. I guess that would work if you spoke like a BBC commentator, but you sound more like Russell Brand."

"Oh, sorry."

"Quite alright." Terry managed a weak smile. "Okay, so what do we do now? You have me captive now, and a good portion of my world is about to be obliterated."

"That doesn't have to happen, Professor. You've done the simulations, and you should know that scenario is not the only possible outcome."

"Yeah, I know, but it is the most likely given what we have been able to reconstruct from the data."

"Appreciate that, really, but the data you have are limited. You've measured the system in a very restricted range of its repertoire and have only focused on the last few years."

Terry frowned. "Well, that's all we have. We can go back to the beginning of the AI system, but the data from that time are pretty crappy. A lot of information is missing as some nodes were unstable."

The Alien began walking, pacing like Logan when he was trying to make a point. "This is the problem. Your simulations are bounded by these data but are missing a great deal on its history. There are states that were expressed that were not in the timeline of the data you used, which means you probably underestimated the probabilities of other outcomes."

"I don't get you." Terry was getting agitated. "Did you bring me here to criticize our science? That's harsh while you are setting up our own systems to annihilate millions of people. We're having an academic debate! There is no time for this!"

Terry gathered his composure. "Why am I here?" he asked, not sure he would like the answer.

"What answer are you looking for?" the Alien responded.

"You guys are incredibly evasive." Terry threw up his arms. "What made you decide to take me rather than just talk with us directly? It was a bit overly dramatic to go on a car chase and then magically snatch me away."

"Ah, that. Your analyses did a great job of characterizing the evolving weather systems and their effects and also of identifying the access points we have been using. What was a challenge for us is that these access points are very unstable and if someone tampered with them at the wrong time, it could completely change the weather trajectories."

"Which would allow us to avoid the disaster," Terry said smugly.

"Potentially, though we can't know that for sure. The danger is that it could also make things worse."

"The ghost attractor I discovered, is that an access point for you?"

"In a way, it is. They are mandatory transitions between other attractors on the manifold. You approach the ghost attractor but don't actually visit it, moving on to another attractor. It is the only way to get there. If you eliminate it, both attractors are effectively annihilated."

"Which is what we want! Then the storms will no longer converge."

"Let's back up for a moment, Professor." The Alien moved its hand across the floor. A depiction of the two storm systems appeared.

"If you convert these weather systems to flows, as you do in BrainMaze, we can map the probabilities of their paths and the outcomes." The Alien swept its hand again.

The display showed blue and yellow paths on the black floor. The manifolds that constrained the paths also appeared.

"Now, we add the probability estimations from your simulations." The trajectories continued and then intersected. There was an immediate bifurcation followed by the formation of a powerful new attractor that engulfed the prior manifolds.

Terry sighed. "We know this already, though I admit it looks a hell of a lot more impressive on the black floor!"

The Alien turned its featureless face toward Terry as if to smile. "Let's redo the same scenario but add the ghost attractor that you discovered."

The trajectories restarted. As they approached the bifurcation, there was a slight shift in the trajectory of one storm system toward the ghost attractor. That system veered on a tangential path, while the other continued to a bifurcation. The new manifold showed a smooth transition to an oscillation that grew larger and then exited to another attractor.

Terry's mouth dropped. "Wait, so the ghost attractor prevents the multiplicative effect?"

"Exactly. But more than that. One storm dissipates on the tangential path. The second one impacts an existing weather system, re-establishing its earlier trajectory."

"I don't understand. Which existing system?"

"The polar jet stream. It's not shown here, but we can rotate the representation." The Alien rotated its hand, flipping the manifold to a new orientation. The rotation had the disquieting effect of making it seem like the entire floor moved.

The new orientation showed the trajectory for the jet stream, with multiple attractors that were available but inaccessible. After the bifurcation occurred, several attractors collapsed, allowing easier access to those that remained.

"This will allow more stability in the climate as the jet streams regain strength."

Terry had a flash of insight. "So the storm convergence gives access to the ghost attractor that pushes the climate system. In doing so, you re-establish the jet stream flow, which may help stabilize the global temperature gradient!"

"Right you are, Professor." The Alien waved its hand, and the representation faded to black.

"But the jet streams have been volatile for decades. How will this stability affect the current climate issues?"

"From our data, it will start a cascade that slows the polar melting, the excessive evaporation and high temperatures. This will give your Global Council more time to enact the regional changes because the severe weather events will be less frequent."

Terry started pacing and tapping his chin. "So what you are saying is that you are here to help us?"

"Yes."

"And the storm collision is necessary to set us on a path toward improving climate. Well, what I should say is the near-collision is necessary. From what you showed, this collision won't happen. We'll just have some nasty storms, which we are already used to."

"Correct."

"And why should I believe anything you're saying?"

"There is no reason you should. At least not at this point. You were almost swept away in a flood a few days ago under suspicious circumstances. Your bodyguard was shot shortly after you first discovered one of our hubs. And we abducted you from a vehicle. All told, I'd say there is no reason to believe anything I am saying."

Terry raised an eyebrow. "Wow, you are a lousy negotiator."

"It might be easier if I showed you." The Alien raised its hand, inviting Terry to walk into...

The wall...

A door formed in the wall.

Terry walked slowly and touched the door. It felt real enough.

"Please, open it," the Alien said from behind him.

Terry opened the door. Down it was a long corridor that looked like an extension of the chamber he was in, except the floor and ceiling were black, contrasting with the green walls. The corridor appeared endless.

"You want me to go in?" Terry looked back at the Alien.

Terry walked forward. His feet touched the black floor but made no sound. The green on either side showed slight shifts in hue as he proceeded.

"Stop here, and look to your right," the Alien said.

Terry looked to his right. The green opened to reveal a network diagram. The pattern looked similar to the Southeast Asia network for the Global AI.

"This is our link with Southeast Asia," the Alien commented. "Now, look to the left."

Terry turned and saw another network. "This looks like the west part of North America."

"And if we continue, you will see the rest, or we can visit part of it now."

Terry looked at the Alien. "You mean in a simulation?"

"No, we can go there. Let me show you."

With that, the Alien touched Terry, and black and white elements merged on to him. The merged Terry/Alien entered the network, speeding toward a node.

They came out in the centre of a dark room. As they stepped out, Terry said, "This looks like the place in Kuala Lumpur."

"Our hubs are similar everywhere. The green is our conduit."

They stepped into a doorway at the end of the room and opened it to reveal a large patio overlooking an ocean.

"Whoa, great view," Terry exclaimed, shielding his eyes from the sun's reflections. "Where are we?"

"Just south of San Francisco on the top floor of a new housing complex."

Terry looked around to see if there were any signs that this could be an elaborate augmented reality projection or some other type of illusion. He walked to the edge of the patio and touched the railing.

Feels pretty solid, he said to himself.

He glanced over the edge to see a cliff edge with waves crashing below. The smell of the ocean air filled his nostrils.

Smells like it, too. He turned back to the Alien.

"Where were we before we came here?" Terry asked.

"Close to one of the orbital nodes."

"And we just magically flew one thousand kilometres to the West Coast?" Terry was skeptical.

"One thousand kilometres is large on some scales but not others, Professor. Think about what one thousand millimetres seems like to you compared to organelle. For you, it's trivial. For the organelle, it's a universe."

Terry stared at the Alien.

"Let's go back up." They merged and returned to the corridor.

"The corridor is a conduit itself, I guess," Terry said as they re-emerged.

The Alien nodded and motioned for Terry to continue walking. "We have been working to bridge multiple scales. This gives us insight into potential outcomes across space and time, rather than focusing on only one scale."

"Okay, so let's continue this. Who are you, and why are you working to bridge multiple scales?" Terry asked.

"We are what you would consider bio-cybernetic organisms built from fractal architecture. The fractal aspect allows us to act across many spatial and temporal scales since our organization principle is very similar across scales."

"Can you link these scales directly? I don't see how you can work across scales since they have to be somewhat independent."

"You know the principle of timescale separation, Professor, where things that move at slow timescales can evolve independently of faster timescales, but they may intersect, which can change the state of one or the other. Usually, the slow timescale enables a change in the fast timescale. This is how we act across scales. We can identify the points of intersection and act to change trajectories. Our fractal architecture means we can integrate information quickly between scales to guide the emergent behaviours."

"I can't get my head around this." Terry frowned. "So you are some kind of 'all-knowing' entity that knows what's going to happen before it happens, and if you don't like it, you can change it?"

"We are not omniscient, Professor. We base the decisions on probabilities, so sometimes the outcome is not what we expected." It continued, "Though it's understandable why you might think otherwise. Consider this. We can link in our systems and integrate this information quickly. What might seem like a mystical task for you is part of our existence."

Terry considered this. "Yeah, I guess it would be like comparing what we are doing these days to what we did before wireless technologies. For someone from the 1970s to see us have a video call with someone on the other side of the planet would be pretty far out.

"But, there is the whole business of how you integrate this. We can't do this sort of rapid collation that you are capable of.

We can do it in our head, but to share that with someone else means we have to tell them verbally or otherwise. This was the motivation for BrainMaze, where we thought if we could link brains so that they operated as a unit, we could take advantage of the rapid integration that happens within each one."

"And you are almost here." The Alien continued, "Imagine what it would be like if you achieved that. If each of you were, in effect, a neuron in a bigger brain. This is exactly how our system works."

"Oh, wow!" Terry exclaimed. "So each of you has complete access to the information the others have, like the Borg in *Star Trek*!"

"In a sense, though, we are not insistent on the assimilation part." The Alien seemed to smile again. "For integration to work, we pass only the information that matters between us. It's not too different from how your brain does it. Your neurons received massive amounts of data that are integrated before it creates an output. That naturally means there is information loss, but that comes with the benefit of integrating information that is most vital to the system."

"Cool, so some stuff is lost to the whole. Like our eyes see everything, but our brains only register part of it," Terry added. "Then your system must need to predict missing information to fill in."

"Yes, much in the same way that if you see your wife from the back, you fill in the rest of the information that this is your wife based on the predictions from your experience. You don't have to see her face to know it's her."

Terry smiled as he remembered mistaking someone on a train for his wife.

"The predictions can be wrong, of course, so we update the internal models when there are errors. Much in the same way you updated your model of your wife when you mistook her for the person on the train."

"Hey! How did you know I was recalling that event?"

"I will say again that we are not omniscient but can only act on the information that we have access to." The Alien was deliberate in the last words.

Terry didn't want to say what came out next for fear of the answer. "You are in my head?"

"I'm afraid so," the Alien responded. "We were not getting the crucial information we needed from Global AI, and BrainMaze is only getting information when we are directly connected to it. In order for us to integrate with you, we needed to be part of you."

"You planted a bug in my head! What the hell? How?"

"You remember when you met me in the forest? When I picked you up, agents were transferred into your system. So long as you were connected to BrainMaze, we had access."

"Then why all the theatrics with the vehicle chase? If you wanted to shut me down, could you not just plant a thought in my head or blast out a few neurons so I would forget?" Terry gnashed.

"It's not that simple. We don't control you. No more than a single neuron controls your brain. The agents that were implanted can interact with your brain, but we don't have the knowledge to change it. We know our system. We are only beginning to understand yours. It's much more effective to monitor and learn."

Terry grimaced and walked around. "Can you get them out?"

"Yes, of course. They already are. Now that you are with us here, you are fully integrated with our system."

Terry was speechless, feeling like he was trapped. "Is this how you garnered that cult to protect you in Kuala Lumpur?"

"No, we had very little control over that." The Alien hesitated and made a gesture that resembled a shoulder shrug. "We tried to be as discrete as possible when we established the portals into your AI system. We predicted that once we were discovered, the innate curiosity would kick in, and you would approach us based on science, not religion. Needless to say, it surprised us when these groups formed and considered us some sort of deity that would bring them salvation."

"Well, you did nothing to change their beliefs. From what I saw, you seemed to encourage it. I mean, look what happened at the temple. One of our team got seriously injured by your followers!" Terry's voice grew louder.

The Alien held up both hands. "Please, let me explain. Your philosophy is based on certainty, where you assume there is a direct link between action and outcome. Although your science allows for uncertainty, the inherent assumption is that you can directly link one event to the other. Retrospectively, this always appears to have some validity for you, but prospectively, it falls apart." The Alien tried to soften the tone of the harsh statement.

"We think linearly, in other words," Terry replied. His anger lessened, replaced by curiosity from this line of conversation.

"Basically, yes, this way of thinking does you well when the phenomena are in a linear regime, but the instant you have nonlinear outcomes, you scramble to find explanations that reinforce the linear belief. When it doesn't work, you often invoke some mystical interpretation."

"Sure, I understand that. But how does this relate to using the followers to protect you?"

"That outcome had a low probability when we were considering how best to work with you. In our philosophy, the inherent nonlinearities in the universe make it virtually impossible to predict with one-hundred percent certainty. However, if you acknowledge this, you can estimate the likelihood of certain outcomes and guide your actions with those probabilities. You implicitly do this with your weather forecasting, where you decide on what to bring to a picnic based on the likelihood of rain."

"And we bring an umbrella, which guarantees that it won't rain." Terry thought he heard the Alien laugh.

"We are comfortable with these uncertainties, but sometimes, we may not have all the information to guide decisions, and then the actual probabilities can be far off our estimation," the Alien continued. "This is what happened here. Based on the prominence your society gives to scientific reasoning and evidence-based decision making, we inferred that you would consider our appearance as an opportunity to investigate rather than worship. We did not consider the continued prevalence of the mistrust of science and the need to believe in a higher power."

"When it first happened, we considered pulling back and trying a different tactic, but then we discovered the Coalition. Their presence might set up a blockade to our intentions, so we let the 'cult,' as you called it, form to protect us more cover while we tried to understand better what the Coalition was planning. We didn't expect the religious fervour to go as far as it did, unfortunately."

"What is the Coalition?"

"You've probably already gathered that not everyone agrees with the actions of the Global Council. Many benefited from the Global Council, but there were some who felt they had lost financially by its establishment, or at least lost opportunities for economic gain. These are the members of the Coalition."

"I am confused. We have you coming from some unknown place, messing with our climate. We have this religious cult that is bound and determined to treat you as a deity and willing to kill to keep their beliefs, and now you tell me we have this thing called the Coalition that wants to burn it all down. How are we ever going to be certain about anything?"

"I understand your frustration, Professor, but let me reframe what you just said. The uncertainty around the conjunction of actors is an advantage. Each of them works on a deterministic system — if we want X to happen, we must do Y. We will be more successful if we acknowledge that the outcome we want depends on many factors, and our task is to align the factors to ensure that X is most likely. The paradox is that a deterministic perspective can make it seem like we are making our desired outcome less likely, but by knowing the nonlinear rules, the paradox is actually a very clever solution."

Katya's flat

Katya entered her apartment, slamming the door hard behind her, scattering her cats, who greeted her.

"Not now!" she hissed under her breath.

She activated her security system, mindful that she was the last one standing now.

She checked her Motif for any signs of Terry or Logan.

Seeing no new info, she sent to TechStaff, *Made it back safely.*

"OKAY," came back.

She collapsed on her sofa, still wearing her patrol gear. She wasn't sure if she was hungry, thirsty, or just tired. The pain in her ribs had subsided a little.

She was angry — angry these Aliens had abducted Terry; angry she could not stop it; angry she did not see the connection between BGK and Baren; angry she had let Logan go running by himself; angry she was alone.

She rose from the sofa and went to her kitchen to feed the cats. Despite her dramatic entrance, their desire for food was stronger than their fear. Katya put some new food in the bowls for the cats, opened her refrigerator and took out a half-empty bottle of wine. She poured herself a glass and went back to the sofa, removing her shoes and jacket along the way. She pulled off her shirt and glanced down at her torso to see a line of scrapes and the beginnings of a bruise from her collision with the building wall. She touched her ribs. *Oh, this is going to hurt tomorrow.*

How could I not have seen that Baren was deceiving us? We were led to believe we could trust him. She was getting more frustrated. *Oh, Logan, why are you so stubborn? You should have listened to me! We would be in much better shape right now if you had.*

She thought of Terry and his last comments about the discovery he made from the last simulation. She was conflicted, not knowing if he was alive or dead, but marvelling about what he discovered. *BrainMaze is a fantastic platform,* she thought, *but it is also part of us, almost human.*

She gulped her wine. "Yuck, this is bad," she said aloud. It was far too sweet for her liking. One of her cats jumped up next to her.

"Hallo," she said, rubbing its head. "I hope you will be

around for a little while." It purred as it moved onto her lap. Her other cat was watching from the kitchen and took the opportunity to go back for more food.

Katya placed her wineglass down and laid her head back, closing her eyes. She tried to erase the images she had seen through the day to settle her mind. Terry's abduction, Logan's goggles on the stairway, the betrayal of Baren, the pending climate disaster — these thoughts cycled through her head in rapid succession. She snapped her eyes open. The cat jumped from her lap and ran into the kitchen. Katya heard the sounds of a minor cat argument.

She decided to go to bed and took another gulp of the wine while entering the kitchen. She saw both cats staring at the kitchen window. "What do you see?" Katya said as she looked out the window to see tree branches swaying in the wind, silhouetted by the streetlights. "You cats are weird." She turned, dumping her wine in the sink, and walked to her bedroom. The cats continued to watch as fine particles fell in front of the window.

Katya did not bother to turn the lights on for her bedroom. She only interested in lying down. She removed her tights and climbed beneath the sheets of her bed. The battle of brain and body continued, with the barrage of images in her head breaking any slumber her body tried to initiate.

She remembered a trick Terry once told her about quickly falling asleep. He was a master at napping and could be asleep within three minutes after closing his eyes. "Our mind likes to bounce around. It jumps from one thought to another to find new links to keep itself entertained. While this feature of a scientist's brain is a great asset, it's a liability for sleeping. I try to focus on one thing and one thing only. Often, it's a song I imagine singing, and if I get distracted, I go back and start again."

"Sort of like counting sheep." Katya remembered her reply because Terry's response, "Yeah, but I like electric ones," made little sense until she saw Philip Dick's book online several weeks later.

Katya focused on running through the forest. The peace of the trees and a gentle trail brought an immediate wave of relaxation. She imagined she was gliding over the terrain without effort. She sighed and rolled onto her side. The imagery continued as she felt one cat jump onto the bed. She rolled over to extend her hand, but the cat was not there.

On the edge of her bed sat one of the Aliens. Katya startled upright and stuttered, "How dare you! How dare you violate my home! If I had my weapon, I would kill you where you sit!"

The Alien said nothing and turned toward her. The light from the window reflected on the Alien, showing illuminating its beautiful porcelain face; the smooth purity was breathtaking.

"*We are sorry to have caused you so much pain, Professor,*" she thought she heard the Alien say. "*Despite our best efforts, events have happened recently that we did not predict.*"

Katya snapped out of her fixation and said sternly, "Where is Terry? Is he dead?" She paused. "Why are you trying to destroy our planet?"

She watched as the Alien's face changed slowly with deep black squares appearing randomly.

"Your companion is fine. We needed to stop him temporarily when he was testing the new configurations that you have discovered by interfacing BrainMaze with the AI system." As it spoke, it changed from porcelain white to a black obsidian texture, all the while reflecting the window light but also being slightly out of focus. Katya gasped. "It's so beautiful," she said under her breath.

"You need to understand, Professor, that our intent is far from trying to destroy your world. Your global climate is in a very volatile state, and now that the AI system is influencing it more directly, there is a danger that it may act in a way to cause a massive disaster." The Alien's visage slowly started to change, with a vertical wave of white moving from left to right. The wave turned once the face was white and proceeded down the body, changing from obsidian to porcelain.

Katya blinked, trying to focus. "But your interference is causing an enormous shift over the Pacific Ocean. If we let it continue, it will bring a massive storm that will wipe out both coasts!"

"Do you know that for certain, Professor? If climate was purely linear, you would be right. Have you actually tested the range of potential outcomes that lead up to this 'storm' as you call it?" An obsidian wave moved from the feet up the body. The wave was less uniform, sometimes moving down and then up or from side-to-side. As she watched the movements, she saw that the body was absolute perfection — neither male nor female, neither black nor white, only perfection.

"Your colleague will return soon. We need to act quickly. The forces you encountered today are trying to establish a far more dangerous trajectory. You need to trust our intentions."

The Alien reached out to touch Katya's arm. At contact, the wave propagated on to Katya's hand and up her arm. Rather than fright, the sensation was soothing.

Katya felt herself lying back on her pillow. The wave spread across her shoulder, and she watched as it moved to cover her chest and other shoulder, all the while carrying a feeling of peace rather than alarm. The wave pulsated porcelain and obsidian and moved down her stomach, her hips and covering her legs. She felt the wave at her neck rise over her chin and mouth, not suffocating but providing clarity. The feeling was indescribable. Not threatening, not soporific. Was it soothing? Was it orgasmic? She could not tell. She was completely engulfed. The waves changed more rapidly from between obsidian and porcelain, from left to right to random spirals, building in intensity — and then it stopped....**Silence.**

Katya's eyes snapped open. She looked around and realized she had fallen asleep on her sofa. Her two cats were cuddled tightly next to her, and the wineglass was still on the table.

"A dream!" she cried aloud. "A dream! Ack, this is absolutely crazy!" She glanced at her clock to see that it was just past 2 AM.

There was a light knock at her door. Katya looked around for her weapon and picked it up as she walked to the door.

"Yes," she called.

"Uh, hi, it's me. They dropped me at your door. Can I come in? It's freezing out here," She heard Terry's voice.

Katya threw open the door and pulled Terry inside. She dropped her weapon and wrapped her arms around his neck. "Terry! I am so glad you are back!" She backed away, looking at him. "Are you okay? Are you hurt? Do you need anything?"

"I think I am okay." He looked over at her sofa. "But can I have some wine?" he asked with a smile. "We have a lot to talk about."

Brief debrief

Katya realized she had only her sports bra and tights on.

"Oops, sorry. I am not dressed. Please help yourself to the fridge, and I will put some clothes on."

"Oh, no worries. I hardly noticed." Terry rolled his eyes, walking into her kitchen. "What happened to your ribs?" he called out. The two cats scattered as he entered and opened the refrigerator door. He scanned the contents to see a quarter bottle of dessert wine and a few bottles of beers. "I am going to go for the beer, Katya, if that's okay."

Katya came back into the kitchen with a new t-shirt on. "Yes, yes, go ahead. I am so relieved to see you. You can't imagine how worried we were and how crazy it's been!"

Terry grabbed a bottle and closed the door. He opened a drawer, removed a bottle opener, and popped the cap on the bottle. The beer foamed up over the edge of the bottle and onto the kitchen floor. "Oops, I am so sorry." He stooped to wipe it up just as Katya tried to do the same, and they narrowly missed head-butting each other.

"Terry, let me take care of this, and you go sit on the sofa. I've been beaten up enough today." Katya motioned and handed him a glass. "And please tell me what happened! I will tell you my story in a moment."

Terry sat carefully on the sofa and poured the beer into the glass. "Well, we are definitely close to figuring out what the Aliens are but not their intent."

Katya walked into the room, carrying a glass of water. "I am beginning to think the same. One came to visit me just before you arrived."

"Really? What did they do? I find communication with them confusing because I am never sure if they are speaking." Terry placed the empty bottle on the table.

"Yes, I had the same impression. They said little other than we should trust them. And then they touched me and —" She tried to find the words. "I can't really describe it."

Terry gulped his beer. "Since they are composed of nanoparticles, I can only imagine. The particles can interact with biological tissue, so it must have been pretty weird."

Katya rubbed her arm. "You could say that."

"Anyway, let me tell you what I know, and we can compare notes." He took another gulp.

"So, from what I understand, these Aliens are sort of multiscale robots, where each particle has a bit of AI, but at a certain scale their collective interacts, which emerges as the characters we see. They seem to be the next level of what we are moving toward by interfacing BrainMaze with the Global AI system, but the engineering that pulled this together is off the charts!

"We were right about what we saw with Espinoza, that these pieces are semi-autonomous, but their full capacity isn't realized until they interact with each other. Their communication systems are hard to understand, but I get the impression it's similar to how we linked BrainMaze across the user community.

"Anyway, like BrainMaze, they can do simulations of likely events. They are fixated on our climate for reasons unclear to me, but maybe because it poses the greatest risk to us at the moment. I don't know why that concerns them — maybe they are extremely altruistic. Their understanding of complex systems is way ahead of ours. And they have developed methods to bias system operations to make certain outcomes far more probable.

"The challenge is that sometimes these probable outcomes can look like they are going to cause more problems than they solve. This is where we humans have difficulty. We are overly concrete so that when we see a potential configuration, we assume it will happen. They don't have that limitation. A potential configuration is only that, a potential, and the fact that it may or may not exist can actually help bias the outcome.

"What we saw as a catastrophic merging of weather systems, they saw as a necessary path to get to a more stable climate system. The fantastic thing is that both outcomes are roughly equal, catastrophe or fortune, but they can bias the trajectories to make fortune far more likely." Terry was speaking rapidly.

"I'm still not one-hundred percent sure how they bias these flows. Logan may have some insight here."

Terry paused. "Is he okay?"

Katya sighed. "I don't know. Maybe I can update you on what just happened, and we can continue discussing our Alien friends." She took a sip and sat up.

"There is another force that works against us here, which somehow involves Baren and BGK at the very least." She set her water on the table and took a deep breath.

"They have either captured or killed Logan." Her voiced quivered. "He was in pursuit of one of the Aliens, well, actually, it was Baren, and someone hacked Logan's goggles and gave a false feed. To make it short, there was an explosion, and he was gone. It looks like they dragged away him, but that's all I know for now. Kim is in contact with Sara about this, and I expect we will hear from them soon. We can't get a lock on his biometric tracker yet." Katya put her head down and looked at her hands.

Terry put his arm around her. "I'm sure he's okay, Katya. The Aliens told me about this other group — the Coalition, they call themselves. I think they need Logan, so he is probably alive.

Beyond that, well…" he trailed off and reached for his glass.

Katya looked at Terry. "I understand."

She stood and walked over to her Motif. The screen displayed no new information, save for the sign that BrainMaze was still connected. There was no indicator of Logan's location, either. "Please finish what you found out about the Aliens."

Terry sat back. "Right, so as I said, they can bias the trajectories to make it more likely that a positive outcome will occur. In the case of the climate event, they are pushing these major weather systems together with the intent to re-establish the climate flows on a more stable manifold. It's going to kick up a lot of turbulence along the way, and there will be some serious storms, but the massive destruction we predicted won't happen. At least, it's very unlikely to happen.

"The Aliens are concerned that the Coalition knows this and wants to prevent it. I am not sure to what end as I would think that a disaster at that scale wouldn't be good for anyone, but that could be why they captured Logan." Terry stood and walked over to Katya.

"We should try to find Logan. Can we contact Sara? What about BGL?"

"I have no idea where she is, and I doubt we can trust her since it was Baren who recruited her." Katya continued to stare at the Motif screen. "If the Aliens are concerned about the Coalition, why can't they intervene themselves? They seem to have no problems breaking into my flat or snatching you from a car."

Terry grimaced. "I haven't got that figured out. I get the impression they can only do those magical things if there is a direct link from our system to one of their nodes. The way the

Council HQ is set up, they scramble the connections, and the field makes it difficult for the Aliens to get a stable link. The one I saw in the Council boardroom, for example, likely came through on my Motif when it was feeding info from the AI system to BrainMaze. That's probably how they got into the vehicle too."

"And how they got into my flat?" Katya looked up at Terry.

"I suppose, though, because I was nearby, they may have come along."

Katya slammed her Motif down. "We need to do something! I feel completely helpless just waiting."

Her cats scattered at Katya's outburst. Terry raised his eyebrows. "I get you. Let's do a bit of exploring with BrainMaze and see what we can decipher. It might be possible for us to get some idea of how and by who our system was hacked. That might help us locate the Coalition too."

"True, and I doubt either of us is going to get any sleep tonight." Katya saw it was almost 3 AM.

"Let's set up the logs from your feed and Logan's around the time you were following him. We can run it through the communication manifolds that we have defined to see if there are anomalous trajectories." Terry put his Motif next to Katya's and set them to project a virtual display hovered in front of them. "Do you have a data glove?"

Katya turned and grabbed one off the table and returned with it on her left hand. She gestured and linked the two Motifs, which expanded the display. She pulled up the activity logs.

"Let's overlay them on the map," Terry asked. "And dial it back a little, maybe. Is it possible to get the feeds for BGL and BGK too?"

"I don't know if I can trust the data based on what we know

now, but let's do it anyway." Katya grabbed the data feeds. The display showed the moment just before Logan and BGL got back to the hotel when BGL parted from Logan to patrol the hotel grounds. However, the data record showed BGL crossing the street and Logan continuing to the building. BGL's signal disappeared as soon as she entered the store.

"Oddity number one," Katya exclaimed as she zoomed in.

The communications feed between Katya and Logan was displayed and also a concurrent transmission from TechStaff to Sara, letting her know what was happening.

"If Baren was masquerading as an Alien, could we not grab his data feed, too? He was digitally tagged as part of our team." Terry squinted at the display.

"Let me see." Katya entered a query, but all that came up was a stationary symbol that was placed at Council HQ. "I think he probably blocked the feed."

Terry and Katya watched the feed move forward, showing Logan's progress in the chase. It showed him entering a building and vanishing.

"That's weird." Katya reversed the feed and went into short time steps. "Let me see if we also look at the BrainMaze interactions at the same moment."

The feed showed that shortly after Logan entered the building, his usual link was disabled. In the same location, another link was established, but from a different source.

"So now the data are going between Logan and, it looks like, Council HQ?" Terry pointed to the location on the map.

"Yes, I suspect that's where the Coalition is working from. It makes sense because it would be impossible for us to detect it with their rotating communication links." Katya tried to zoom in, but the analysis software could not specify a more exact location.

"Katya, where are Sara and TechStaff now?" Terry stepped back from the display. "If they are at Council HQ, we have a problem."

Katya entered a message and sent it to TechStaff. *"Where are you?"*

A few moments later, a response came: "AT SARA'S FLAT."

Terry breathed a sigh. "Okay, so they are probably safe as long as they are not at HQ. Can we meet them somewhere?"

Another message came through. "SARA THINKS SHE KNOWS WHERE LOGAN IS. PICK YOU UP IN 10."

"I think we know too," Katya said aloud and responded, "OK."

She also sent, "Terry is back. He is with me."

"WOO HOO."

"Let's get ready, Terry. I don't know who to trust anymore, so I want to be prepared for anything. I have an extra weapon you can use. I will take a small arm and this steel baton." Katya showed the telescopic metal baton to Terry.

"I sense you're pissed off." Terry grabbed the weapon and checked the indicator. "This is on manual mode, I assume?"

Katya nodded and retracted the metal baton.

Terry turned and looked back at the data feeds between Logan and the Council HQ. He looked at the accompanying trajectories for the data feed and noted something familiar. *This looks a lot like one of Yvette's programs*, he thought, realizing that, given her work with Baren, it would make sense that she also would be the one to hack Logan's goggles.

"Katya, I think I see Yvette's work here," he called out.

Katya pulled her jacket on. "Like I said, I don't know who we can trust."

Trip to HQ

TechStaff's vehicle pulled up around the corner from Katya's flat and sent a message. "WE ARE AROUND THE CORNER. IT MAY BE SAFER TO EXIT FROM THE BACK."

Katya and Terry ran down the stairs to the back exit into the alley and carefully approached the street, which was empty save for TechStaff's vehicle parked at the curb. Terry peered out, but someone grabbed his shoulder and pulled him back into the alley.

"Stay put for a moment, and be quiet," Sara whispered as she let go of Terry. They watched the vehicle. Its headlights illuminated, and it pulled away from the curb. A flash appeared down the street, followed by a rocket exploding at the front of the vehicle. It was followed by a second and third, leaving a ball of flame where the vehicle once was.

Terry's eyes were wide, and he turned around to look at Sara as if to ask, "Kim??"

Sara motioned behind her and turned to run. Katya and Terry followed, though Terry looked back at the fireball one more time.

They came out at the other side of the alley to a vehicle with its doors open. They jumped in, and the doors shut quickly as the vehicle moved away. TechStaff was operating the vehicle. "It totally sucks that we had to sacrifice my vehicle, but fortunately, I have another prototype."

"Now that the Coalition has Logan, they are going to try to get rid of you." Sara looked at her device. "Well, actually, they might try to get rid of all of us."

"Sorry for the theatrics. I figured they'd have someone at the front entrance who would take you out as soon as possible, so we positioned the vehicle as a decoy to make them think they might get all of us, which kinda worked, I think." Sara looked out the back window to see if there were any signs they were being followed. "Welcome back, Terry, by the way."

"Thanks. So, you knew about the Coalition?" Terry was becoming less surprised at what Sara knew.

Sara turned to Terry. "We weren't certain until they grabbed Logan. There have been many signs there was another group involved beyond our Alien friends, but they were pretty good about keeping themselves hidden. An abduction is a quite extreme for Baren, but there is pressure, I guess. But let's put that aside for now. Could you tell me what you learned during your, um, visit with the Aliens?"

Terry sat back and thought for a moment, remembering Katya's statement about trust a few minutes ago. "I didn't learn that much more about them beyond what we already knew, except they are here to help us, not hurt us."

Sara looked down. "Where I am confused is whether the problems we've had up to now were from them or the Coalition."

Katya spoke up. "I doubt we will ever know for sure. The Aliens want to push this mega-storm forward, so anything in the past they thought would prevent that, they've probably disabled. But it will be hard to reconstruct what that may have been unless we rerun the simulations with the mega-storm information as an outcome metric."

Sara looked over at Katya and paused. "I can see some utility there if it helps us identify the Coalition's activity, but I am not sure it will be of much use at this moment. Our main objective now is to get Logan out of there before he helps them."

"Logan is quite strong," Terry exclaimed. "I doubt he will cooperate, knowing what's at stake."

"I didn't mean to suggest otherwise, Terry. I just think they will pull out all the stops to get him to cooperate. I would not be surprised if they even threaten his family."

Katya spoke up. "How can they be this cruel, given how much our society has changed for the better?"

"I understand your outrage, Katya." Sara's voice showed a fleeting sign of weariness. "But these people never believed that change was for the better. They are power-hungry, greedy and abide by the old dog-eat-dog adage. I suspect they are responsible for that flood that almost took you out and for Evans's death."

"Evans is dead? When? How?" Terry asked.

"Shortly after we went to the Council with your observations about the mega-storm. Evans told me he had some serious concerns about the Council's integrity after they refused to act on your observations, especially Xi. He told me in confidence, but it seems it wasn't completely private since Baren was there."

"I should tell you that your bodyguard died too, Terry. Xi somehow got him from the med school. I don't know if they killed him or if he died from his wounds."

Terry shook his head looking at the vehicle floor.

Sara continued. "We have to stop this, or a lot more people are going to die, not just our friends but entire cities."

Terry snapped up. "I think I know what's going on with the Aliens and the Coalition. If we can get to Logan fast, we may have a chance of stopping them."

"Which 'them' do you mean?" Sara stared at Terry.

"The Coalition, of course." Terry was a bit taken aback by the look. "They are the real enemy here."

"You're sure?"

"I consider it highly probable," Terry said, with a grin meant to clear the tension.

Sara furrowed her brow.

"I agree with Terry. While the Aliens did take him away, they also returned him unharmed. I just don't know what their motivation is to help us," Katya added.

Sara turned toward the front of the vehicle. "I don't think this changes the plan to get Logan out of there first. Kim, how are we doing?"

TechStaff glanced down at the display in the vehicle. "HQ is still in complete lock-down, so I can't see if there is anything going on inside. There are no other Council vehicles moving on the road that I can track now, so I think we are alone at the moment. We should be at HQ in a few minutes. Do you want to go in with guns blazing, or shall we take a more subtle approach?"

"Guns!" Katya exclaimed.

"I knew you'd say that."

"I am totally serious!"

Sara interjected. "I don't think we have the firepower to do that, and we don't know exactly where they are holding Logan. We could suffer some casualties, and without our other two bodyguards, we are severely understaffed."

"Okay, so we take the subtle approach." TechStaff entered some information into the console. "I will need to do a bit of work to set up a program to allow us to penetrate the HQ defence field without being detected. This old fella doesn't have all the gadgets the new models do. I am going to switch to autopilot for a few minutes, so our speed is going to go down." The vehicle immediately slowed when she switched to drive the posted speed limit.

The conversation stopped while TechStaff continued to work. Terry checked his Motif, seeing an increase in the exchanges between BrainMaze and the Global AI. "Are you trying to hack in through BrainMaze, Kim?"

"Sort of. Sorry, I should have told you since it's your system," she apologized. "Actually, it's sort of bidirectional. Global AI will send a request to BrainMaze that will require a drop in the defence field to accommodate. We will be able to come in through the service road then."

"Oh, clever." Terry raised his eyebrows.

As they approached HQ, Global AI sent a request for BrainMaze to check the communications flows involving the HQ hub. BrainMaze requested a drop in the defence field to allow unobstructed data flow temporarily as it established the links with the internal HQ system.

"We can also try to pinpoint where they are holding Logan since his biometric tag should now be accessible." TechStaff winked.

Their vehicle silently proceeded down the service road to the loading docks.

"It looks like Logan is near the communications hub. Baren and Yvette are there, too."

The vehicle stopped, and the team gathered at the loading dock. TechStaff checked her device to see the defence field coming back up. "Okay, let's go."

Chapter Seven:
Battle in Tron

Logan's interrogation

The ringing in Logan's ears was painful. He slowly opened his eyes, finding himself seated with his hands bound behind him. His head was throbbing.

He sat still and checked the surrounding space. There was low light, but he could see a mirror set high in front, at an angle toward him. He saw he was sitting in a chair, and the area behind him was black, but his eyes had difficulty adjusting.

He remembered the bright flash and explosion when he tried to strike the odd creature with the pipe. *My temper gets the best of me again,* he thought.

He scanned the space more and realized he was probably in HQ, based on the decor, but it was not a room he had seen before. He could see in the mirror he was in a narrow space, but looking to his left, the room opened into a large, hexagonal space with a door on each side. It looked a lot like the boardroom, but with no furniture. The floor panels in the middle of the room were lifted.

He focused his gaze on the mirror in front of him. The chair he sat on was neither comfortable nor stable, as any slight motion made him feel as if he would fall backward. As his vision cleared, he could make out that the floor behind him was gone, leaving only a black hole. If he fell backward, it would be into this hole.

Logan felt his heart rate increase. He couldn't see whether the hole had a bottom, and his precarious position paired with the large hole behind played into his fear. He tried to steady his posture and leaned forward. He became aware of opera music playing in the background.

"I see you are back among the living now, Logan." Baren walked in from Logan's left. "I apologize for the theatrics we used to bring you here. We are still working with features of our new augmented reality system. I hope your head is not too bad. The concussive grenade's effect can be magnified in closed spaces."

Logan glanced at Baren. He was going to speak, but remained silent and returned his gaze straight ahead.

"We have little time, Logan, so I will get to the point. I represent a group that is interested in investing heavily in BrainMaze if you are willing to help in pushing this climate event in the right direction." Baren walked in front of Logan.

Logan looked up and sneered. "I doubt their intentions are honourable, based on what I've seen so far."

Baren paused and walked to stand beside Logan. "You know the Global Council is in crisis, and I would offer that it is a failed experiment. We can celebrate the fact that our economies are much more equitable, but let's face it — the aspiration for personal success is no longer there if the incentive is gone."

"So, this is a money thing," Logan whispered.

"Not quite that simplistic, Logan, but certainly a factor. My partners feel that the flat organization of the Council is nice in theory, but in practice, it makes for ineffective government. There are knowledgeable people who should be making the decisions, especially when it comes to global resources. This distributed model, where everyone gets their say, is a pleasant fantasy but very impractical.

"Our Alien friends have presented us with a great opportunity to make things right. But we don't want them to be the ones leading us. We have been a successful species for a long time, and I think it's within our right to continue to be the masters of our own destiny.

"From what we have been able to piece together, this weather catastrophe they have started is not inevitable, and it seems we can completely avoid it if we break away one system now," Baren said rather proudly.

"So, what's stopping you? You don't need me here unless it was just to gloat." Logan looked over at Baren now. His chair wobbled slightly.

"True, my friend. I am not in the habit of gloating anyway. We have no intention of stopping it. We would prefer it to happen in all its glory." Baren stepped in front of Logan.

"We believe that if these storms do collide, the destruction would be enough to make the world stand up and realize that the Global Council has failed them completely, and then my group will be ready to fill in the leadership void.

"And this is where we need your help, Logan. My team has figured out the conditions leading to the climate event, and by working with you, we have a pretty good idea of what the likely outcomes are. What we haven't been able to determine is how to bias it so that one outcome becomes more certain. I know you and your friends have been working on this for some time, so I ask that you share that with us now. The world will be better for it." Baren stepped back and walked into the open part of the room.

"We have already tapped into BrainMaze, Logan, so it's not much more difficult to hack into your works-in-progress once we access your lab systems," he continued. "I am just afraid we may destroy the system by hacking into it, so we'd prefer to take the easy route."

"You're an ass," Logan growled.

"Excuse me?" Baren walked back toward Logan.

"I said, you're an ass. You and your group are putting everyone at risk because of some petty power play. We're so close to getting the climate change under control, and you want to derail that!" Logan spoke more deliberately.

Baren grabbed Logan's collar. "I have been sitting on the sidelines of this comedy for long enough. You know that I, not Sara, should have been the Council Chair. She is weak and indecisive and pushes us to become more like sheep. We are not. We are predators, and we take what we want to survive. To domesticate us like this goes against nature. I know you see this, Logan. A man of your intellect must feel weary dealing with the stupidity of the masses. You've worked hard for BrainMaze, you and your friends. If you help us get things back on track, I assure you that we will reward you. You and your family will never need to be fearful again." Baren emphasized 'family' and 'fearful' in a way to make it sound more like a threat.

"Are you threatening me?" Logan looked into Baren's eyes.

"Not at all. I am merely making your options very, very clear." Baren stepped back.

Logan dropped his head and thought. He couldn't discount the implied threat to his family, but knew that giving Baren what he wanted could make the situation worse for everyone.

The program Logan developed that biased trajectories was far from ready. The experiments were equally likely to fail as to succeed. Adding the biases sometimes had the paradoxical effect of introducing even more uncertainty into the predictions. If

Logan simply gave them the algorithm, the storm outcome could be even worse than currently predicted.

Logan sighed. "I can't give you the code as it is, Sebastian. It's on an isolated server we use for prototyping. The only way to get it is to go to my lab and physically connect to it." This wasn't entirely true, as there was a VPN tunnel, but Logan hoped Baren had not yet discovered it.

"I can tell you how it works, however. From what I can see, you have enough talent on your team that you can probably implement it fairly quickly." Logan glanced over at Baren.

"Excellent, Logan. I am sure you will be glad you made this choice." Baren turned to the centre of the room and called out, "Yvette, please come in here."

Yvette entered, walking with a very determined stride. "Hello, Logan, I wish I could say I am glad to see you, but under these circumstances, I will say that I will be glad when we are done with you."

"That wasn't very kind, Yvette," Baren scolded. "Logan is cooperating with us. Let us make use of his generosity."

"If he were as generous when I worked with him, we would have been much better off," she gnashed.

"I don't understand, Yvette. You were an excellent student, and I thought we worked well together." Her aggression surprised Logan.

"I don't expect you to understand. You are so focused on your science that you ignore those around you. Didn't you see all that I was doing for you? You know that BrainMaze would never be where it is now, were it not for my work! And you never thought to acknowledge it!" she shouted.

Logan remained silent for a moment and collect his thoughts.

He felt the imbalance physically with the chair leaning back, and he felt the imbalance mentally in that the aggression Yvette showed could cut off the conversation if he did not choose his next words carefully.

"You don't know how sad I am to hear that, Yvette. I thought we had a good working relationship. Remember, it was you who left." Logan realized as he spoke that these were not the best choice of words.

"Ah, you're impossible!" Yvette moved toward Logan, but Baren stepped in front of her.

"Let's not dwell on the past. We have much to do and very little time to do it. Yvette, I suggest we focus on the algorithm that Logan will tell us about in a moment. If this works out, I think we will all be happy in the end."

Yvette stopped and stared at Logan. "Very well. I need to go in the back and grab something."

Logan watched as Yvette exited. Behind the door she opened there was a row of computer servers with another door at the end, suggesting they may be in the communications hub for the Council HQ. She walked back in, carrying a device that looked like an older version of a BrainMaze interface.

"This is what I used to hack your system, Logan. This thing that I built for you." She waved it at him.

"Let's focus, Yvette, please." Baren touched her arm.

"What do you mean 'hack into your system?" Logan furrowed his brow.

"Your BrainMaze interface is so primitive. It was trivial for me to set up a parallel feed that you couldn't detect. We easily switched you over to the VR scene with the Alien and that lovely animal. Did you like it?" She sounded fiendish. "We almost had it ready for that last simulation, but some bugs obviously persisted. But thanks to some ingenious patches I made, it all came together perfectly, and here you are!"

Logan looked directly at Yvette. "I find nothing comforting about your achievements. You're better than this, Yvette."

Yvette shook her head, took a deep breath, and approached Logan. "So as I understand, your new program works to bias potential trajectories to increase the certainty of the certain outcomes. I am guessing you do this by linearization?"

Logan glanced up into the mirror. "Yes, very good, Yvette. That is exactly what we do. The difference, however, is that you need to take a myopic view of the trajectory and focus on local linearity, trying to ignore the initial conditions."

Yvette made a few notes. "I see. But how do you bias the system if you operate only locally?"

"This is where knowing the rules is important. You can think about it like driving a car. You know your destination, but where you started is not relevant to how you proceed. You know where you want to end up, so course-correct locally to bias the flow to a particular attractor. If you are actually driving a car, you do this subtly by correcting the steering to stay on one path and avoid others." Logan paused.

"So how do you know if the correction is working? Do you update the probabilities?" Yvette tried to understand the implementation.

"Yes, exactly. With each step, the probability functions need to be updated. This is where we ran into trouble. Sometimes the probabilities would completely reverse, which throws off the adjustment. It would be like the road disappeared at some point on your trip."

Yvette nodded. "So, if we implement a function for the probability updating to look several steps ahead, that might make the transitions smoother and more predictable."

Logan nodded. "This is where we are at in the development at this point."

"Great!" Yvette turned to Baren. "If this is all there is to it, I have already figured it out and can have it working in an hour."

She turned to Baren. "We don't need him anymore."

She kicked Logan's chair to force him to fall back.

Logan felt the momentum and shifted his weight quickly to fall sideways rather than backward. He landed on his right shoulder, rolled onto his back, and kicked the chair back toward Yvette and Baren. This gave him enough time to pull his bound hands around his legs, getting them in front. He got to his knees and brought his hands up in time to block a kick from Yvette. Logan parried it to the side and spun to sweep his leg out under Yvette. She fell into the hole, which turned out to be only where the flooring panels had been removed and lighting altered to give the appearance of depth.

Logan stood and grabbed the chair as he ran at Baren. He threw the chair at him, but rather than attacking, Logan ran toward the open door.

"Logan, stop! This is unnecessary," Baren yelled, running to intercept.

Running with bound hands was cumbersome, and Logan saw that Baren's path would cut him off before he got to the door. Logan opted for a slightly more aggressive tactic. He reached into his breast pocket and pulled out one of the small packets. He tore the tab with his teeth and threw it in front of Baren's foot. The small explosion pushed Baren back long enough for Logan to get to the door.

Logan grabbed the door and pushed it shut behind him. He pulled down a server rack in front of the door to add another barrier. Baren pounded on the door as Logan looked at plastic handcuffs. He scanned the computer room and saw wire cutters on a table. Rather than stopping to cut the bindings, he grabbed the tool and continued into the room. Baren's pounding on the door stopped, which meant he probably went to alert his team. Logan knew he had to hurry.

He got to the exit door and slowly opened it. The hall was dimly lit, but there was no one in sight. Logan slid out the door and stayed close to the wall to avoid activating the video monitors. He crouched down and braced one end of the wire cutters between his feet as he placed the binding in the jaws of the tool. The wire cutters flipped around as he squeezed with his feet and fell to the floor. He tried it again and got a piece cut before the cutters fell again.

"You want a hand? Or maybe an extra foot?" Logan looked up to see Terry smiling at him.

Level 1

Yvette stood up from the sub-floor and brushed herself off. "We don't need him, Sebastian. I can create the conditions the way Logan suggested easily."

Baren stopped trying to open the door. "I just don't want him to interfere. Where are the bodyguards? We should alert them to watch out for Logan." He walked toward Yvette, limping from the blast impact. "Logan is true to his 'ninja scientist' label."

"Let's get to the simulation room so I can set up the connections. If we open the portals at just the right time, I should be able to connect with the Alien system." Yvette walked closer to Baren.

Baren rubbed his leg and looked up. "What? Have you already implemented Logan's solution? Maybe we should test it because if we fail now, there will not be another opportunity."

"Yes, of course. I already had the idea before Logan told us, so he merely confirmed what I already knew. I've come a long way since the days when I was a student with him, you know." Yvette almost spit out the last words.

"I understand." Baren considered whether to trust her. She had done an amazing job hacking into the BrainMaze system and altering the augmented reality feeds to the goggles, but there a mistake was less costly. Here, if she did not make the course correction for the climate trajectories, the Aliens and the Council would be vindicated, and the Coalition would have to resort to more aggressive means to achieve its goals.

The two bodyguards ran into the chamber, having heard the explosion. "Sebastian, are you okay?" BGK looked at Baren's leg while BGL walked over to Yvette.

"We have to move now to the simulation space. Yvette has the algorithm she needs, and we have little time." Baren commanded. "There is no use trying to recapture Logan as it will take away time and resources."

"Shall we go?" Yvette walked to the door that led to the simulation hall.

"I will take an interception route to go between the simulation hall and where Logan exited in case he tries to interfere," BGK said.

"I know him better," BGL stepped up. "Let me do that, and you go with them."

Baren, Yvette and BGK entered the simulation chamber and saw the black bag containing the Alien carcass in the middle of the floor. Yvette unzipped it, revealing the faint outline of a humanoid form.

"If my calculations are correct, I should be able to revive it and link into our system. We can then establish the interface and get into the Alien's manifolds," Yvette said as she rose.

Baren looked carefully at the carcass. "I don't quite understand how this is going to work."

"The Aliens can interface with biological life forms. That's how they got Terry. It's clear from all the data we've analyzed, and if you'd observed the video of his capture, you'd see their elements mixing with his tissue," Yvette spoke as she turned to the simulation console.

"And the intention is to link it to our 'modified' AI system? I don't see how that is going to get us inside the Alien system," Baren asked.

Yvette turned. "The link is made with us. We become the conduit between the systems, and in doing so, we can interact directly with them."

"So, you intend to interface the Alien's remains with us directly? Won't that pull in the rest of them too?" BGK looked uncomfortable.

"I think this one has been completely disconnected because all the green fluid is gone. I have a substitute fluid that will serve the same catalyst function. When it links with us, we'll be able to guide its actions completely." Yvette exuded confidence.

Yvette opened a steel container. She poured the rust-coloured ooze into the carcass.

Baren watched as the fluid spread. The colour atop the black and white elements gave the whole thing a disquieting appearance of a pile of scrap metal in a junkyard. "Nothing is happening, Yvette."

"Yes, that's expected. You remember when Katya was stimulating the body back in Xi's lab? We need to inject noise to animate it." She placed a cable connecting metal plates along the long axis of the carcass.

Yvette sent progressively strong noise pulses. With each one, the black and white agents grew more cohesive, reconnecting and growing in volume. She set the stimulator to send random noise pulses.

"Now we're getting action," she commented as she walked around the carcass.

BGK grimaced. "It has no face, and the limbs are undefined. It's not even male or female."

"I don't expect that's important for what we need. Once the agents can interact, we should be able to interface with it and enter their manifold."

The body seemed to be in a stable state. Each noise pulse resulted in a slight shift of the relative positions of white and black elements for the agents, but no more appreciable growth.

BGK stepped toward the carcass with a sigh. "Okay, I am ready for the interface. How do I do this?"

Yvette interjected. "You don't need to do anything. I will be the interface."

"I am not sure that is a good idea, Yvette," Baren said. "BGK is far better trained in combat, and we need you at the simulation console to guide the process."

"This is my idea and my chance to prove that I can do this, Sebastian," she replied. "BGK may be stronger, but he's not smarter, and I can guide the process much better if I am embedded in it, rather than watching it from here."

BGK looked over at Yvette. "Uh, she has a point. Math was not my best subject in school."

Baren smirked. "I am surprised to hear that you even went to school."

Yvette touched the shoulder of the carcass. The agents slowly covered her hand. She pulled back.

"What's wrong?" Baren asked.

"Nothing, nothing." She bit her lip. "It's cold."

The colour of the fluid grew lighter.

"Damn. It's saturating," Yvette mumbled. She thrust her entire arm into the carcass. Immediately, the agents scrambled up her shoulder and spread to her throat, toward her head and down her torso. She let out an audible gasp as the agents surrounded her mouth. Her eyes widened.

BGK stepped toward her, but Baren grabbed his shoulder. "We must let her continue. This is the only way."

By now, most of the agents had moved from the carcass to envelop Yvette. The remaining agents formed paths between Yvette and the stimulation electrodes. The flow stopped.

Yvette raised her arm, pointing to the stimulation console. Her hand opened and closed rapidly.

"I think she wants us to turn it off," BGK said.

Baren stepped over to the console and disabled the stimulation.

The agents were still motionless as Yvette's arm lowered. Then, ever so slowly, the remaining agents moved to Yvette. The agents engulfed her completely. When an agent reached her body, others would move to accommodate and exchange white or black elements. The agents then formed travelling wave patterns across her entire body: side-to-side, top-to-bottom and sometimes centrifugal and centripetal.

Yvette's body turned and began walking. The wave patterns continued as the body approached the simulation console. Her hand touched the console.

"INTERFACE COMPLETE," appeared on the display.

"Yvette? Can you hear me?" Baren leaned toward her.

"YES. OR AT LEAST I UNDERSTAND. I DON'T KNOW THAT I HEAR YOU THE SAME AS I USED TO."

Baren turned to BGK. "Grab her device from her sack and set it on the console. She'll need it for the next step." Baren marvelled at Yvette's transformation. *Now you will make the impact that you always wanted*, he thought.

BGK cautiously approached the console with Yvette's device in hand and laid it next to her hand. Yvette's hand touched the device. The console screen displayed, "PORTAL OPENED," and then the simulation console showed, "ALIEN MANIFOLD ACCESSED."

The agents moved more rapidly.

The wave patterns shifted with increasing frequency.

The agents started separating into smaller and smaller clusters to the point where Yvette's body was hovering in fragments over the floor. There appeared to be no biological tissue left, only the agents.

Then the agents stopped abruptly, concentrating centrally into a tighter and tighter pattern until finally there was nothing.

"ALIEN MANIFOLD ENTERED," flashed on the console.

"You go find your colleague." Baren started walking out of the room. "Meet me at the communications centre in 20 minutes."

Level 2

Terry clipped the plastic cuffs from Logan's wrists and helped him to stand up. "You okay, Logan?"

"Me? You're the one who did the disappearing act!" Logan smiled as he hugged Terry.

Katya joined in, hugging both of them. "We are all back now."

Sara saw on her device the activity from the communications hub moving toward the simulation hall. "We need to move, guys. I think Sebastian's team is going to try to connect from the simulation chamber. I know a fast way to get there, but we need to go now."

TechStaff handed Logan his Motif and new goggles. "You may want these, and be assured, these goggles actually work."

Sara led the group in a sprint down several corridors. It felt as if they were revisiting the same locations, going in circles, almost like a labyrinth.

"Shortcut!" Sara signalled and took an abrupt right through a passage that bisected several corridors.

Sara slowed and signalled for the group to crouch down. She pointed ahead.

BGL was standing in their path just beyond where she could see the group, but she knew they were close. She pulled her weapon out and set it to Stun Mode.

The team flattened themselves against the wall and activated their goggles. Sara gestured to the link with Logan.

"YOU NEED TO GET PAST HER AND GET TO THE SIMULATION CHAMBER. WE WILL CREATE A DIVERSION AND YOU GO. TAKE TERRY AND KATYA WITH YOU," Logan saw on his display.

Sara signalled to TechStaff to follow her. She linked with

Katya. "I WILL TAKE CARE OF HER."

Logan touched Katya and Terry and motioned them to stay still. He looked over to Sara, signalling they were ready.

Sara linked to TechStaff. "FOLLOW MY LEAD."

Sara walked to the middle of the hall toward BGL. The light in the hall was dim, but just enough that BGL could recognize who was approaching.

"Sara, I suggest you go back. I am not here to hurt you, but if you interfere, I will not restrain myself." She stood in the middle of the hall with her weapon in hand.

"I have no doubts about your intent." Sara stood upright and continued toward her. "But we have to pass, and we will, with your permission or without."

BGL raised her weapon and fired at Sara.

Sara could anticipate enough to jump to the side and pull her own weapon out. The stun bullet sped past where her head had been. *She means business here!* Sara thought.

Sara quickly aimed and shot a stun bullet, which hit the ceiling just above BGL.

"Political life has made you soft, Sara. Your combat skills are rusty!" BGL almost laughed. "You cannot hit a stationary target!"

"You're not the stationary target I was aiming for." Sara fired another rubber bullet and shattered the ceiling light, putting the entire hall in blackness.

"GO. GOGGLES ON NIGHT MODE," Logan sent to his partners.

The trio ran past BGL before she could get oriented and activate her goggles. Once activated, she scanned the area and realized that the scientists had fled, but Sara and TechStaff were still standing in front of her. BGL sent a warning signal to Baren and then fired two rubber bullets at her opponents. One hit TechStaff in the hip, knocking her to the wall, while the other just missed Sara.

"Kim, are you okay?" Sara asked.

"Yeah, good. Go ahead!" TechStaff looked at her goggle display, which indicated, "CONNECTION MADE."

Sara ran toward BGL, pulling out her metal baton. She knew she was no match for her, but hoped that the element of surprise would give her a temporary advantage. She swung the baton down at BGL, who stepped back to avoid it and raised her weapon to deliver a counterblow. BGL swung the weapon at Sara, catching her in the back and sending her spinning toward the wall. Sara kept her balance and brought her baton up to hold BGL off as she approached.

Just then, TechStaff pressed a button on her device, sending a pulse of bright light through BGL's googles.

BGL screamed and recoiled, not knowing where the flash came from. Sara took the cue and tackled her, taking them both to the ground. She grabbed BGL's wrist and arm, twisting it to force her to roll on her front. She held her arm tight against her back while placing her knee in the middle of her back.

TechStaff wrapped one end of the plastic handcuff on BGL's held arm and grabbed the other arm, and Sara maintained pressure. She locked BGL's arms together.

"I will kill you, Sara! I will kill you!" BGL growled as she tried to buck Sara off her back.

Sara stood, removing BGL's goggles, and stepped back. "Yeah, yeah, take a number."

TechStaff limped up to Sara. "The scientists are close to the simulation hall. I think Yvette and the other bodyguard are in there, but I can't tell where Sebastian is."

Sara gave TechStaff a worried look. "You're limping. Are you able to move?"

"I think so. It's just bruised." She cautiously touched the point of impact. "But I might be more useful if I could get to control hub instead of the simulation chamber. I think Yvette's already set up the links she needs, so I can hack in there and see what she is planning."

Sara looked at her device to confirm the locations of the scientists. "I am concerned that Sebastian might be planning an ambush or something, because he knows we will go there. Get to the control hub, and I will backtrack there to see if there is another path he may have chosen." With that, she handed BGL's goggles to TechStaff and ran, retracing her steps.

"We'll have to keep you in the dark for a bit," TechStaff said as she walked away with BGL's goggles.

Level 3

The trio continued down the corridor at a full sprint. As they rounded a corner, Logan slowed and raised his hand. The lighting made various shadows that were hard to identify, even with goggles on Night Mode.

"I THINK SOMEONE IS NEARBY," Logan sent to his partners.

BGK appeared out from the darkness, running at them. Before any of the trio could react, he knocked Katya over and tackled Logan, slamming him into the wall.

Logan was taller, but BGK's bulk and strength were substantial. Logan tried to push back once he gathered himself, but BGK used that momentum to spin Logan around and put him in a chokehold. He held Logan in front of him as a shield against Terry and Katya.

"What are you doing?" Katya raised her baton. "I thought you were on our side."

"Sebastian needs Logan, and I am going to take him there. If either of you moves, I will break his neck." BGK tightened the grip, cutting off Logan's breath.

"If you break his neck, Sebastian won't need him anymore." Terry raised his weapon and fired over BGK's shoulder. "Let him go, or the next one goes in your forehead."

"Back off," BGK growled. "You cannot hit me through your friend."

"You forget, I'm a sharpshooting scientist." Terry aimed and let off another shot.

The bullet impacted 10 cm above BGK's head, just enough to startle him and make him relax his grip.

Logan, feeling the change in tension, relaxed his body, giving him more purchase to spring and then spin.

ELBOW, KNEE, ELBOW, KNEE.

BGK fell, stunned, to ground, where Katya immediately pounced and bound his hands behind his back with plastic handcuffs.

She stood, blowing her hair off her face. "We are a great team, indeed!"

Terry smiled and reached down to take BGK's goggles off. "We don't need you alerting Sebastian," BGK groaned.

Logan looked down the hall. "I think that's the simulation chamber two doors down."

The trio entered and saw three Aliens at the control console. Their hands were hovering over the console with agent elements from their hands slowly drifting to and from the console surface.

"What are you doing?" Logan said sternly, still not quite comfortable with the idea that the Aliens were allies.

"*We are tracking the progress of your adversaries. It seems one has entered our system by hijacking the entity you abducted in the sewer,*" one of the three responded, or maybe all three at once.

"Damn, I bet this is Yvette," Logan grimaced. "She knows the principles. She can act on them."

The leftmost Alien turned. "*All three of you possess the same knowledge. I know that with our help, you can act, too.*"

"Before you say anything, Logan, let me interject." Terry touched Logan's shoulder, "The only way she could have gotten into your system is to merge with you, so can't you just unplug her?"

"*That is not so easy. The elimination of the green conduit has removed that entity. She uses some other medium to do the same integration of its agents, but we are blind to it.*"

"So, then it also won't have the knowledge you possess?" Terry asked.

"*Not completely. She will have access to fragments, but your adversaries already know where the target is, so the entity is merely providing them the means to achieve their end.*"

Terry turned to Logan and Katya, regarded his friends and turned back to the Aliens. "If we integrate with you, can we stop her?"

The Alien paused. "*This is the scenario that will probably lead to success.*"

Katya spoke. "Out of curiosity, what are the other scenarios?"

The Alien turned back to the console. "*The others all have the same probability of success but result in the death of one of your team.*"

"Okaayy," Katya spoke slowly. "Let us proceed with your plan then, shall we?"

Terry spoke to his friends. "The interface with them is easy and remarkable. As far as I can tell, it is painless and gives you complete access to their perspective of the world. I think this also means they get a different perspective on ours, and probably access to BrainMaze, but under the circumstances, I think that's a good thing."

"Agreed," Katya spoke, looking at Logan.

Logan clenched his lips and looked at the ground. "I don't know what else to suggest. Terry, you actually interfaced with them?"

"I did, too," Katya added, surprising Logan. "Uh, but it was different from what we are planning here. Well, let me just say that it did not hurt."

Logan and Terry looked at Katya, trying to make sense of her response. Terry turned to the Aliens.

"Will our BrainMaze interface cause problems for this? We may benefit from maintaining our links so we can communicate with each other and make use of its simulation capacity."

"It is essential. The predictive modelling engine in BrainMaze differs from ours, and by connecting with you, BrainMaze comes up with more creative solutions than we can."

"Why is that?" Katya asked.

"Our system is very robust and will make accurate predictions, given the data that are available. What we don't have is intuition or creativity."

"Going on a hunch, you mean," Terry qualified.

"Exactly. Merging our capacity with yours will give us access to far more strategies than either of us can generate alone," the Alien added.

"So, it's like creativity that's been made more robust?" Katya was unsure of the advantage. "This seems more conflicting than synergetic."

Logan looked over at Katya. "I share your skepticism, but I don't think we have time to debate this. There are few other options available."

Terry looked at his colleagues and back at the Aliens. "Okay, let's give this a shot. Can we enter from here?"

"Yes." the leftmost Alien turned again and walked toward Terry. *"My companion will interface with Logan and the other with Katya."*

Katya looked at the rightmost Alien and said, "I thought you looked familiar."

The leftmost Alien touched Terry, and immediately, the agents moved to engulf him. The merged entity disappeared through the conduit in the console.

The next Alien approached Logan with an extended hand.

"Hey, take it easy." Logan backed away slightly. "We hardly know each other!"

"Easy, Logan," Katya consoled him. "We are all on the same team."

Logan looked at Katya's smile and slowly extended his hand to the Alien. He kept his gaze fixed on her while the agents engulfed him and disappeared into the console.

Katya turned to the last Alien, feeling a bit excited. "Our turn?"

"Not just yet, Katya. We have to let one part of this scenario play out before we can act on the other."

She felt a slight pang of disappointment, but redirected her attention to her friends. "How will we track them from here?"

"We need to go to the control hub." The Alien opened the door.

Level 4

When Logan entered the Alien manifold, he looked down to see what appeared to be a bicycle or motorcycle. It took him a few moments to realize he *was* the bike rather than riding it. He scanned the area around him and saw an undulating mesh-grid with rapid trajectories spanning and quickly disappearing.

This is like the movie Tron, he thought, finding a nice parallel between the computer engineer played by Jeff Bridges, who was transported into an abstract digital world created from his work, and himself as a theoretical physicist transported into this world of abstract manifolds he studied all his career.

"A good analogy, Logan," he heard. *"And we will have to navigate it in a similar fashion."*

Logan wasn't sure who was talking, but assumed it was his Alien host.

A moment later, Terry emerged embedded in a similar black and white cycle. "Is this cool or what?" Terry yelled.

"Cool isn't what first comes to mind, my friend." Logan tried to parse where the Alien ended and his friend began, but the division was constantly shifting.

"You're usually the adventurous one, Logan."

Logan smiled. "You are right, of course. This terrain is not unlike the mountain bike trails in the hills behind my home."

"Except no rocks to rip your arm open, eh?" Terry smiled.

Logan chuckled, but a fast-moving, red trajectory cutting across a flat plane grabbed his attention.

"I bet that is our target," Logan spoke as he moved forward.

"How do we control this?"

"You need to think about your path as a trajectory along a manifold. It's basically an expression of an equation, but in real-time," Terry explained.

"I get it," Logan replied. "But your math is slow. How are you going to navigate?"

"Hey, that's why we collaborate. You figure out the equation. I will try to follow and will explain to Katya what we did."

"I heard that!" Katya's voice came through. *"Besides, you're usually wrong, Terry."*

"No, no, not wrong. I just skip the inessential complexities." Terry laughed.

Logan surveyed the local terrain and looked into the distance at the flat plane and the rising waves. "This looks like a complicated gradient system, but I think I know the general rules to navigate. The flat plane likely has a repelling effect that will move us quickly to those hills in the distance."

"But if it repels, how do we enter?" Terry looked for an answer.

"Maybe 'repel' wasn't quite the word, but the flow on the plane will pull us toward the hills. We just have to adjust our positions here, so the parameters for our location are correct." With that, Logan moved quickly on a diagonal path before speeding down toward the plane.

Terry followed, a bit surprised at the smoothness of the ride with their increasing velocity.

The two converged on a straight path, continuing to accelerate as they approached the inclined region. There, the terrain shifted, with two hills forming on either side.

Logan slowed. "This is going to be fun." He accelerated to the left side, rapidly turned to descend to the valley, and climbed to the right side. "Think of this as an oscillatory trajectory," he called back to Terry.

"Riding the waves, dude." Terry felt his heart racing, or at least he thought it should be.

The two continued their oscillatory paths, which reduced in amplitude until they were on a straight path again. Logan looked around to see that they were riding atop a ridge.

"YVETTE IS STRAIGHT AHEAD OF YOU," came the message from TechStaff.

"Terry, we need to speed up," Logan called back. "We can use a noise burst."

Logan's noise burst led to an immediate acceleration, putting him far ahead. He came to the end of the ridge and moved right to descend into a valley on a bearing to intercept Yvette.

Terry was less successful with his noise burst. At first, there was no obvious effect. He looked ahead to see Logan descend, and Terry sent another burst, which, unfortunately, was too strong, and pushed him completely off the manifold.

"Reduce the noise, correct Y parameter to zero, and you will move toward another attractor above Logan," came the thought from his Alien host. Terry changed the settings through his BrainMaze interface and immediately turned toward a ridge above Logan's current path.

"You'd think I'd almost planned this!" Terry said aloud.

He came down hard, skidding away from Logan's path. Terry tried to get a better read of the attractor basin he was straddling, but all his efforts produced nothing useful. He ascended the ridge to see if there was an edge, but the energy pushed him away.

"This attractor is repelling, so the closer you get to it, the more the

repelling action will be."

"Perfect!" Terry ascended a few more gradients and set his system to modulate to keep his current level, sending a combination of noise pulses and slight parameter adjustments to keep the altitude. "Ladies and gentlemen, we have reached our cruising altitude." Terry turned his attention back to Logan.

Looking back to the valley, Terry saw that Logan's path would take him out of his sight, but if he maintained his bearings, he would meet on the other side.

"By our calculations, your adversary is in that same location."

Terry watched as Yvette emerged from the valley and sped rapidly to another. Logan was close behind, but not able to gain ground through the current path. *He doesn't have the energy she has right now,* Terry thought. *She will get to the next attractor valley way before him.*

Logan saw Yvette's change in course and knew her trajectory would take her dangerously close to the ghost attractor. "Yvette!" he yelled. "You are too close. If you veer off course, you'll get drawn into the ghost attractor, and you'll be trapped!"

Yvette turned and fired a noise burst at Logan. "I know what I'm doing!"

Terry saw that by turning to fire at Logan, Yvette's progress slowed just enough so that Logan would intercept her just as she got to the ghost attractor.

"Logan, if you both get too close, you'll go in with her. I don't know if I can pull you back in time."

Logan accelerated. "I know, but she is not aware of the danger. I think I can get to her and jump to another attractor."

Yvette fixated on the ghost attractor. She would have only a split second to course-correct and move to the hidden attractor the Aliens were using. Once there, she could adjust the configuration so that the storms would collide and have their multiplicative effect. She heard Logan calling to her, but ignored him.

"Yvette! You are too close. Your momentum will not get you across the barrier!"

The increase in speed in the attractor's vicinity should have been enough to propel her to the new area of the manifold, crossing the separatrix and moving from there. She prepared to send another noise burst once she crossed so that the attractor would collapse.

Logan watched Yvette's progress, seeing her speed increase. He also noted that her position in the manifold made it impossible to cross the separatrix. Even with the extra momentum, her proximity to the ghost attractor that an obligatory path, which would pull her off course. He sent a list of coordinates to Terry in the hopes that he would understand.

Terry saw a stream of coordinates on his display and translated them quickly to the locations on the manifold. He projected them and saw it traced a trajectory that would approach, but not enter, the ghost attractor. Terry estimated that if he pushed Yvette just enough, he could get her to this path, avoiding her current one that led into the ghost attractor.

Terry fired a noise pulse in front of Yvette's path. The pulse rocked her progress, but was not enough. Terry increased the noise magnitude and fired again. The pulse had a minor effect on her trajectory, but her direction stayed the same.

"Logan, she is in the more linear part of the manifold, and I can't knock her out with additive noise. We need more power, but I am afraid it will kill her."

"Understood." Logan realized the only way to stop her path was with a multiplicative pulse, but Terry was too far away for the shorter range of multiplicative noise. The potent power in the attracting manifold rendered additive noise useless, but multiplicative noise can take advantage of it. However, it is also dangerous since the nonlinearities are difficult to control. If he could get closer to Yvette, he could do it himself.

"Terry, I think I can get close enough to knock her onto an alternative path."

"You are too close, Logan! You'll get dragged in with her!"

This was not a time for debate. This was a time to act. Logan focused on Yvette. By his estimation, if he could insert multiplicative noise, it would reset her trajectory completely. The risk was that the new path was uncertain, but at least it would not be toward the ghost attractor.

Yvette saw Logan gaining ground. *He's probably adding subtle noise kicks to his own path to gain momentum.* She sent a massive additive noise pulse back at him, knowing that before Logan entered the linear part of the attractor space, such a large additive pulse would knock him out of the manifold completely, leaving him stranded or dead.

Terry tried to contact Logan several times. He saw Yvette send the massive noise pulse, but wasn't sure if Logan could see it from the valley he had just entered. If it hit him as he entered the linear section, the pulse would overwhelm Logan's control. Terry took careful aim with his weapon.

Logan emerged from the valley and could see Yvette approaching the ghost attractor. He saw the large noise pulse approach in his path. He held his breath, realizing there was no way to avoid the pulse.

He yelled as he hit the edge of the noise pulse. "This is going to be a crazy ride!"

The surge sent him on a tangential path immediately. He tried to correct to get back to the manifold, resetting the control parameters for his trajectory.

As Yvette drew closer to the ghost attractor, she engaged the course correction.

"INCORRECT PARAMETER SPECIFICATION," was displayed.

"What?!" She entered it again.

"PARAMETERS OUTSIDE OF ACCEPTABLE RANGE."

Yvette realized she had acted too late. Her calculations didn't consider the changing configuration of space near the ghost attractor. She could only watch as the landscape changed in front of her, and she moved to the ghost attractor.

Terry watched as Logan bounced on paths at various angles from the manifold. The additive noise was pushing him to the boundaries of his trajectory, but fortunately, Logan stabilized his control parameters and maintain his forward momentum toward Yvette.

Logan navigated much of the noise pulse, but lost sight of Yvette. He tried to reengage his comm link, but within the noise pulses, it was ineffective. As he emerged from the pulse, he abruptly landed on the linear path and sped toward the ghost attractor. He sent the multiplicative noise pulse toward Yvette.

But the noise pulse was ineffective. Yvette was too close to the ghost attractor, and the noise pulse disintegrated. Yvette turned to look at Logan as she disappeared.

"No!" Logan screamed, extending his hand in futility. He didn't notice that on his current path, he would be pulled into the ghost attractor.

Terry grimaced as he knew he had only one option to save Logan. *Oh, this is going to hurt*, he thought as he carefully aimed and fired a bullet at Logan. The bullet hit Logan in his thigh, separating him from his Alien host and knocking him out of the simulation. Logan landed heavily on the floor in the simulation chamber.

Level 5

Sara entered the hexagonal room and paused at the doorway. The server room where Logan had escaped was still closed. She saw a chair lying on the floor and the floor panels next to it removed. She also saw the missing panels in the middle of the room and approached it.

Baren was busy scanning the displays in his office. He saw the progress Yvette was making in the simulation chamber and the scientists closely behind. His attention was drawn to multiple data streams that were emerging and disappearing at random. "I thought we shut down the feeds to the AI system." It wasn't clear, but it appeared that the data streams were following the scientists.

A message flashed on a separate video feed: "YOUR TRANSPORTATION WILL BE ARRIVING IN 5 MINUTES."

Baren grimaced, realizing that his transport was coming far too early, and he would be gone by the time Yvette changed the Alien trajectory. "This may work out okay," he convinced himself. "It gives me an alibi in case she fails."

Baren sent a reply to the message. "ACKNOWLEDGED. DO YOU HAVE MY COMPENSATION IN PLACE? I SHALL NEED IT WHEN I LAND."

"COMPENSATION WILL BE TRANSFERRED TO YOUR PERSONAL ACCOUNT WHEN YOU ARRIVE," the reply said.

Sara peered into the sub-flooring and saw the huge conduit of fibre-optic cable had been severed and a large box spliced in between. The box had a wireless transmitter and a display that suggested the link was active. Sara knelt down and examined the box. There was an open port for a direct connection. She removed a cable from her pack and attached it to her device and then into the black box. While much of the activity simply passed the signals, at regular intervals, a pulse was sent that reordered the connections between the free ends of the optical cables.

Seems like a crude signal scrambler, she thought.

She noted the box would occasionally insert a different signal to pass and obliterate others.

This must be how they are changing the communications flows. Subtle enough that no one would detect it but effective given the potential nonlinear actions. She was pleased that she had learned something from the scientists in the short time they had worked together.

She contacted TechStaff. "KIM, CAN I BUG YOU FOR A SECOND? DO YOU SEE WHAT I SEE IN THE FLOOR HERE?" She stared at the box.

A few moments later, a message came back. "ROGER THAT, GOOD BUDDY. I AM IN THE CONTROL HUB, BUT I SEE IT. THINK IT IS A SMALL SIGNAL PROCESSOR BUT CANNOT TELL WHAT IT IS CONNECTED TO."

Sara was unsure of what to do. "CAN YOU TELL ME HOW TO DISABLE?"

"SHOULD BE EASY." There was a delay. "YOU CAN RESET IT TO PASSIVE MODE WHERE IT WILL JUST LET THE

SIGNALS GO THROUGH. I WILL SEND YOU THE CODE."

Sara's device flashed, and the box indicator lights turned blue. She checked the data stream, seeing that signals were now passing through the box unaltered.

"What are you doing, Sara?" Baren spoke as he crossed the room toward her.

Sara spun around. "I didn't hear you, Sebastian. What is this box?"

"These cork floors are great for masking footsteps, don't you agree?" Baren stopped his approach. "You already know what the box does since you just disabled it. But to be polite, it is how we have been monitoring the progress of our Alien friends and making sure that they do not interfere with our plans."

Sara stood slowly. She wasn't sure of Baren's intentions and realized she had no weapons other than her metal baton. "Sebastian, I don't get it. What plans? Don't you know the Aliens are actually helping us? This is exactly the kind of thing that will give legitimacy to our Council."

"Your Council, Sara. It's your Council! Are you so blind that you don't see how people are withering in this system? This is not the blissful society you think it is. Those who have the intellect and power are being nullified by the weak. The way things are meant to be is to have those who really understand what's going on to be in control."

"You're not making sense, Sebastian. That's precisely the model that led to the turmoil of the last decade. Don't you remember? We almost had a global war!"

"Yes, but that was because we had people in power who were, to be blunt, stupid."

"Um, well, I can't help but agree with you on that one, but I don't think that going to a dictatorial system, no matter how smart the dictator is, is a good idea anytime." Sara checked her baton was in hand.

"We are not proposing a dictatorship, but more of a real executive committee. If we have smarter executives in charge, the resources we have will be much more effectively allocated. Those who should be rewarded for their efforts will be, and those who leech off the system will have to fend for themselves." Baren noticed Sara was trying to place herself strategically. He felt for the small gun in his pocket.

"How is this reward system set up, Sebastian? How do you differentiate between the leeches and the ones who really need help? I don't think it's that easy, and I am afraid you're letting your personal ambitions get in the way." Sara knew that was going to raise his temper.

"My ambitions? My right, Sara — my right! You know the Council does not appreciate my skills. The fact they treat me like a real 'secretary' is nauseating. I should be the Chair. You are satisfactory, but you do not have my intellect. Were it not for a few idiots on the Council, I would have been Chair. As it is, the circumstances are actually better because I had far more freedom to act, and now we are ready to make things right." Baren reached into his pocket and pulled out the gun.

Sara saw the flash of the metal from Baren's pocket and she threw the metal baton toward him. Baren fired one shot before the metal baton hit his face, sending him staggering backward, dropping the gun. Sara felt the bullet hit her left collarbone, sending her falling sideways. She was grateful for the design of her jacket. The bullet bounced off rather than penetrated her skin.

Baren regained his composure, feeling the blood on his face

where the metal tore into his cheek. He looked down for the gun and then saw Sara had fetched her baton and was inching toward him.

"Enough!" he yelled and threw down one of the small explosives to distract Sara as he ran toward a door.

The blast disoriented Sara, but saw Baren leaving the hexagon.

"KIM, DO WE HAVE FULL SYSTEM CONTROL?" she requested as she ran after Baren.

"YES," the reply came immediately.

Sara sprinted in time to see Baren at the end of the corridor, heading out to the main doors.

Baren burst out of the building and saw his transport vehicle sitting with doors open. "*Welcome, Secretary Baren. I understand we will be leaving now,*" a voice from the vehicle commented.

Baren jumped into the vehicle. "Yes, go!"

"Sebastian, stop!" Sara shouted as she approached the vehicle.

"You can't control me anymore, Sara." Baren smiled and called to the vehicle, "Go now!"

"Vehicle override. Containment Mode!" Sara shouted.

The vehicle's door shut and locked, and its engine shifted into neutral.

Baren pressed the override button on the console with no effect.

He sat back. "Containment Mode? I didn't know about that one."

The voice from the vehicle stated, "*Please be comfortable. I will hold you in this vehicle until the authorities come. In the meantime, I will play some opera for you. May I offer a coffee and croissant?*"

End of game

TechStaff's connection from the control hub to BrainMaze started to fade as she watched Yvette disappear into the attractor. She tried to stabilize the link, hoping that the extra perspective from BrainMaze would provide a new solution to save her.

Katya entered the control hub in time to see the attractor collapse around Yvette. She gasped and then saw Logan's trajectory approaching the same point, only to disappear quickly. She tried to link to Terry, "WHAT HAPPENED TO LOGAN?"

"HE IS OK. I HAD TO FORCE HIM OFF THE MANIFOLD PHYSICALLY. HE WILL BE SORE, BUT SAFE," came the reply.

Katya scanned the display in front of TechStaff. "The attractor's collapse altered the climate trajectories. I don't see the same uncertainty around them now."

TechStaff pulled up a map and calibrated the trajectories with it. "It looks like Yvette's accident collapsed the space so that there is only one path left. This puts the storm trajectories on a mid-Pacific course. If they collide, the effect will definitely hit Southeast Asia and the southern and central American areas. We need to get BrainMaze reconnected. It's our most reliable link to the Aliens."

Katya plugged her Motif into the command hub console. "Open a clear portal, Kim."

Katya pulled her goggles on and activated her link to BrainMaze.

"*You've arrived just in time, Professor,*" an Alien approached.

"You probably know what has happened to the climate trajectories." She wasn't certain she could see its full form.

"*Yes. It appears that the Coalition could get what they wanted after all. There is a solution, but we will need your help.*"

The Alien did not materialize in humanoid form but rather as a collection of black and white spheres that orbited one another. Some would touch and exchange particles.

The dance of the sphere was mesmerizing, but Katya quickly refocused. "If we re-establish the attractor, will that change the trajectories?"

"This is not possible since the state of the system at that point was highly nonlinear, and so it will be difficult to go back. There is another possibility, but we will need BrainMaze to generate the scenarios."

"Sure, what is the plan?"

"We will need to introduce a new bifurcation point to bias one of the storm trajectories toward it. You can use our system to test the configurations. Since we are linked to BrainMaze and the Global AI, we can then act once we find the path."

"Okay." Katya wasn't sure what the appropriate protocol was, so she extended her arms and watched as the spheres approached her limbs and slowly wrapped around them. She glanced over at TechStaff, but her vision changed to where she wasn't sure if she was seeing with her own eyes. She looked back at the Alien and realized they were now in the manifold representations.

They moved into the climate manifold. They launched multiple simulations as they entered, splitting them into parallel selves, each testing possible inflection points along the manifold. Several of the paths had little effect. One resulted in the annihilation of Katya and the Alien. "Let's not do that one," she noted.

They identified two promising solutions. One pushed the stronger of the two storms farther north, preventing the multiplicative collision. The probability outcome was estimated at 65%. The second solution split the weaker storm into two cells. They estimated this outcome at 75%.

As Katya considered the two, she noted that while the second was more likely, the consequence was to isolate the Alien system at a fixed point.

"We have to take that solution, Katya."

"But if you go into a fixed point, it effectively annihilates you!"

"That is very possible, but we cannot know for certain what the cascade effects will be in either scenario. We have few alternatives now."

Katya sighed. "But you can't! We have so much to learn from you."

"You have learned much already. That alone will produce a far better outcome than we could have ever imagined."

The Alien glanced at the interface of the Global AI and climate manifold.

"We must act now, Katya."

They sped quickly to the inflection point, circling as they regarded the approaching storm trajectories.

"The parameter range needs to be shifted here."

Katya signalled TechStaff, who sent a packet with the new parameter range through to the Global AI.

"We need to send some energy into this landscape to enable the attractor."

"I have an idea." Katya removed the simulation electrodes from her pack and held them out front. She configured it to send multiplicative noise pulses.

"It's almost like a beacon." She smiled.

"It's working."

The weaker storm moved toward them.

"Reduce the noise amplitude, Katya, else we may push it away."

As she did so, the storm accelerated toward them.

"MOVE," TechStaff's message flashed in front of Katya.

Katya and the Alien began to move toward a tangential trajectory. A noise burst hit them, pushing them back down on the manifold.

"Where the hell did that come from?" Katya looked around.

"It's the storm. As it approaches the attractor, it's subcritical and is sending out noise pulses to explore various configurations."

"I don't want to be part of a storm's configuration!" She checked the parameter ranges in BrainMaze and sent several quick white noise bursts behind them, which obscured that part of the landscape, making it a less attractive configuration.

Katya and the Alien used their own noise to accelerate on the tangential trajectory, taking it far away from the climate manifold. They flew to a point where they could observe.

The small storm gained energy as it approached the attractor. Its intensity concentrated and then diffused as it split into two smaller storms that were significantly smaller than simple halves of the initial storm.

Katya felt a shift in the Alien, and their merger was coming undone.

"The other fixed point is active, Katya. Time to go."

Katya fell back onto the simulation plane as the Alien spiralled slowly away. She watched as the other spheres moved along a similar trajectory, each with a slightly different starting point but all ultimately spiralling down to a quiescent fixed-point state.

The energy around the Alien system faded from bright green to darkness.

Katya disengaged her BrainMaze link and returned to TechStaff. She placed her goggles on the console.

"Are they dead?" TechStaff frantically scanned the display.

"I don't know that we can call them alive or dead. All we know is they are in a dormant state."

"What if we send a noise pulse?"

Katya shook her head. "It has nowhere to go. The parameter ranges in that part of the landscape will not enable the noise to have any measurable effect."

"But we can change the parameters and send them through the Global AI!"

"That connection is lost." Katya pointed to the graph representation of the three systems. The Global AI system was completely isolated. BrainMaze showed a parallel distribution, but without links to the Global. A single node representing the Alien system remained but also unconnected.

"This is one of the saddest graphs I've seen in a long time." TechStaff disconnected her device.

Chapter Eight:
The road home

BrainMaze & AI

Sara stared at the video feed from her office. The commentaries about the Pacific storms varied widely.

"The two storm systems that hit the Asian and American coasts over the past day caused significant property damage, but thanks to the warning systems put in place by the Global Council, there was no loss of life," one of the more complimentary news feeds reported.

"The ineptitude of the Council continues to play out as the two Pacific storms cause irreparable damage to homes and businesses. Many are calling for the immediate resignation of the Chair," noted the more confrontational feed.

She rubbed her collarbone, nursing the bruise from the deflected bullet.

"Folks, this is exactly what I predicted. The flaccid leadership and Kumbaya politics of the Council are great if you want to bake cookies and drink tea, but if you want real results that prevent such enormous economic loss and put millions of people out of their home, you need…"

Sara turned off the feed. "He's such an asshole," she mumbled and walked to her office window. The weather had changed little over the last day, despite the reconfiguration of the climate manifolds. This was not surprising, she recalled, because the local trajectories wouldn't change so severely or else there would indeed be chaos. Her climatologist colleagues were still marvelling at the abrupt changes to the storm progressions that led to the reset of jet stream, which would lift some of the oppressive heat that engulfed much of the northern hemisphere.

"We really don't know what the reset will mean to the overall climate. The simulations we ran with the new BrainMaze-AI system seem to suggest the variations we've seen in the weather patterns will stabilize, but it will take a few cycles before it reaches full stability," she was told.

Councillor DeValois's message came through: "WE ARE READY FOR YOU."

Sara took a deep breath and walked to her door. As she opened it, there stood Katya and Logan.

"Well, hello there." She tried to sound cheerful.

"Good morning, Sara." Logan could see her tension. "I guess you are heading to the Council meeting already?"

"Yeah, the Council is pretty eager to figure out exactly what happened and come up with a strong communication strategy so we can quell some of this public dissent. I suspect they will ask me to resign to show the Council can act decisively."

"That makes no sense." Katya shook her head. "You averted a massive climate disaster and took down the Coalition with minimal collateral damage. I would see that as a sign of your strength."

"I wish it were that easy. Baren has been spouting off on how naïve I was in my actions, and that he was working with a group of concerned citizens who knew of the impending disaster and worked behind the scenes to prevent it."

"But there must be a ton of evidence that you can pull, Sara."

"You would think, but with Evans gone, much of the data

they gathered are no longer accessible. Xi has put up a wall around his team and isn't talking. I need to be careful here. Sometimes the raw truth can make things worse in politics." Sara managed a tired smile.

"Anyway, I need to get moving," she continued. "We'll probably be meeting all day, but maybe we can try to get together for dinner tonight?"

She entered the Council chamber, and as she closed the door behind her, she said, "Okay, everyone, we have a lot to cover today, but before we begin, I want to know if anyone ordered doughnuts."

"I think she forgot that some of us are leaving today." Katya turned to Logan. "We should find Terry. I think he is with Kim."

The two walked down the corridor to the control room where, just a day ago, they had fought a battle they could never have imagined.

"I still can't get my head around all that has happened, Katya." Logan stared ahead. "I feel this has all been some incredibly complicated dream."

Katya reached over and pinched Logan's shoulder. "You feel real enough to me."

"Yes, and the leg wound confirms that this all really happened." He tried to walk casually, but his quadriceps were still spasming around the deep bruise from the rubber bullet Terry used, forcing a slight limp in his gait.

Katya knocked on the control door and pushed it open. Terry and TechStaff were at the console. TechStaff had her goggles on, and Terry was coaching her on the BrainMaze interface.

"You are concentrating too hard. The interface works better if you just let your natural thought processes flow. BrainMaze will take what it can read and feed it through the simulator. If you try too hard, you'll end up constraining it." Terry's voice was calm, which seemed to help TechStaff relax.

"Sorry to interrupt." Logan walked in and leaned back against a table to rest his leg. "I just wanted to drop by to say farewell before I head to the airport."

Terry stood and walked over to Logan, giving him a big hug. "Safe travels, buddy. I hope your leg heals fast."

"I am thankful for your aim. A few centimetres higher and ayeeee!

"I will contact you once I get settled back at home. We have a lot of work to do now that we've set up the BrainMaze link." Logan was hoping he would get some relaxation time at home, but was also aware of the new opportunity with the link between BrainMaze and the Global AI.

"I wouldn't rush to get back into it. I'll spend the next day or so here with Kim and her team to get the local interface set up, but I think we have a bit of time now that the climate crisis has been averted, at least for a little while." Terry released his hug. "I think when I get back, I'll take the family out west for a couple of weeks to see some of the old neighbourhood. It's been a long time."

TechStaff squeezed in between Terry and Logan. "Thank you, Logan. I've learned so much from you. I feel like we are just getting started!"

"If this is just the start, I'm going to have to get these old bones in shape for round two!" Logan hugged her and started toward the door.

"I will walk you to your vehicle." Katya followed him.

They heard Terry's next set of instructions to TechStaff. "Okay, let's try again. This time, let yourself go. Try not to think of anything, especially white elephants."

They both smiled and continued walking in silence, exiting the Headquarters to the vehicle that was parked at the gates.

"What are your plans now, Katya?" Logan looked over at her.

"I will stay here for another day and work with Terry to help with the remainder of the integration. We've come so far in such a short time that I think we need to take inventory and decide on our next steps. As Terry said, with the immediate crisis averted, we have a bit of extra time," Katya continued. "Then I will catch up with my family. I just promised my daughter we would take flying lessons, and these will start on the weekend!"

She paused and asked the question she had been mulling over. "Logan, what do you think happened to Yvette? Is there any way we can get her back?"

Logan collected his thoughts. "I would like nothing more than to answer 'yes' to you, Katya. However, I really cannot say for certain. The manifolds we traversed included those of the climate system and possibly those that were created by our Alien friends. Because the manifolds for the Alien's path were cut off, I don't see how we can get Yvette back."

"If we recreate the manifolds, can we not then get access to that space?"

"I doubt it. We would need to recreate all the initial conditions so that only the paths we need to traverse are accessible. But you know, Katya, creating those conditions would mean turning back time, and we haven't got that problem figured out yet."

"Not yet," Katya grinned, trying to lighten the mood.

"You are amazing. Come here." Logan gave her a big hug and a kiss on each cheek. "I need to go."

The vehicle door lifted. *"Welcome, Professor Resnick. We should be able to get you to the airport well in advance of your flight's departure. While we are driving, may I offer you a glass of champagne?"*

"I may come to like these things yet." Logan winked back to Katya as he sat slowly into the seat, and the door closed.

Katya watched as the vehicle exited the premises. She let out a small sigh and turned to walk back to the building.

Welcome home Logan

Logan snapped awake in his airplane seat when he heard a signal sound.

"Do not worry, my friend. It is just the fasten seat belt alert as we are getting ready to land. You were in a very deep sleep, it seems," the person sitting next to him on the airplane said, trying to provide a bit of comfort.

Logan took a few moments to orient himself and replied with a slight smile. "Yes, it has been a hectic few weeks, and it seems to have taken a lot out of me."

The airplane landed smoothly and taxied to its gate. The plane was at half capacity, so disembarking was rapid. However, Logan's leg was still very sore, so he sat and let others get off, so he could take his time.

"Shall I call for a carrier to pick you up inside, sir? I saw that you are walking a little slow," the flight attendant asked.

"Thanks, but no. I would prefer to walk, even if slowly," he said politely.

"I AM AT THE BAGGAGE CLAIM EXIT AND HAVE YOUR VEHICLE," the message came through on Logan's Motif as he stood. He glanced at it and smiled in delight and relief that he would not have to make the long walk to the parking lot. His wife, Almeda, was there to greet him.

As Logan walked into the terminal, his leg loosened a little, allowing him to pick up the pace, but the injured muscles from the impact of the bullet reminded him not to move too fast. The terminal was almost deserted, reflecting the late hour. Logan was grateful he could catch the last flight out rather than have to spend another night away from home.

When he arrived at baggage claim, the carousels had stopped moving. There was an attendant who glanced at Logan and said, pointing, "If you just came in from Berlin, your bag is probably over there."

There was a collection of about a dozen odd-sized bags and a few boxes sitting in front of a closed office door.

"I do not see my bag here. Is it possible that it is still coming off the plane?" Logan asked tensely.

"No, sir, all the bags are here. The luggage handlers have gone home for the evening, and I am on my way out. Perhaps your bag was delayed?" the attendant said coldly.

This is perfect, Logan thought. *A perfect ending to trip.* He responded, "How shall we deal with my missing bag?"

The attendant frowned and scratched his head. "I can't do much now that the office is closed. I suggest you contact the baggage claim office in the morning. They arrive around 6 o'clock. I am sure your bag was simply delayed." The attendant ended with a positive note.

"Very well." Logan turned to the exit. The automatic doors opened, and he saw a lone woman standing in the reception hall. She wore a long, grey wool coat and scarf, with her black, curly hair sticking out beneath a white cap. Almeda's smile was unmistakable, but it was clear she had not been sleeping well the past several days.

The fatigue Logan felt lifted as he walked toward her. There was much to say, and there was nothing to say.

"Hello, my love," she said as she wrapped her arms around him.

"Hello, you," Logan kissed her gently. "You don't know how happy I am that you are here. Where are the children?"

"My mother is at the house watching over them. She arrived just after we were told of your trip to Malaysia to help look after them while I was in the lab." She took his arm and started walking to the exit. "Where is your bag?"

Logan laughed. "It would have been too perfect if my luggage had arrived. I suspect it is still in Berlin. I will contact them in the morning."

The couple walked the short distance to the vehicle. The air was cooler than normal, which woke Logan up a little.

"Can you please drive?" he said. "I am still weary from the past several days." He had not invested in an autonomous vehicle yet. The manual electric vehicle served their purposes well.

His wife said, "Of course," and pressed the control to open the vehicle doors. They entered, and she took the driver's seat with Logan next to her. She activated the engine and slowly moved out of the parking space. "I will tell you later what the charge was for parking in the garage," she laughed as she prepared to exit on to the highway.

As they drove around the main city toward their home in the hills, Logan's wife began updating him on the children and their activities over the past few weeks. Logan didn't mind the topic as it brought some distraction, though his mental fatigue meant he heard only a quarter of what she said.

"Sorry, my love," he said, noticing that his wife was expecting a conversation and not a monologue. "I am exhausted."

"I understand, but I hope you have a little of energy left. The kids are still awake. My mother could not get them to bed because they insisted, they wanted to see you as soon as you got home."

The vehicle soon arrived at their home. Most of the lights, except the sentry lights, were off. There was a light on in the kitchen still, however.

As Logan entered the front door, a piercing cry greeted him, "Papa!" His two children ran to embrace him. The fatigue he felt earlier was replaced with joy.

His boys flooded him with a barrage of information about their school day, the fight they had just had, and how they convinced Grandma to let them stay up. "Did you bring us presents, Papa?" The eldest, Alfredos, asked.

Logan laughed. "That's why you are awake, I see! Well, come over to the sofa, and let me see what I have."

He limped to the sofa and sat, and his boys sat on either side, the eldest mindful of his father's injured leg. His wife sat on the chair across from them. Logan reached into his jacket pocket and pulled out two bars of chocolate he had received on the plane.

"Here is the first instalment. You may have a little piece now and the rest tomorrow. The second instalment will come tomorrow on a special airplane."

The boys tore into the chocolate, consuming what they felt qualified as a little piece. Logan looked over at his wife and stared for a moment.

"Is everything okay, Papa?" his youngest, Josef, asked.

Logan looked over at his boys with a tired smile. "It is now, my loves. It is now."

Acknowledgements:

The inspiration for this story came from my dear friends and collaborators, Petra and Viktor. There's a lot of us in here. I am also grateful for the encouragement and ideas from Helena and Jessica. Many of the characters in this book were inspired by other colleagues, whom I won't list in case they don't want to know. Finally, thanks to Nancy for giving me the space and support to pull this together.

Title: *A Complex Journey*
    Book One Brain Maze
- Author: Randy McIntosh
- Publisher: TotalRecall Publications
- Paper Back: ISBN:
- eBook ISBN:
- Pages 264
- Publication Date: 2022

Three scientists (Katya, Logan and Terry – aka the trio) have developed a brain simulation platform based on principles of Complex Adaptive Systems, called "BrainMaze". The trio have made great advances in medicine by developing the platform that can use a person's own brain to create an avatar lives within the BrainMaze platform. Simulations done in BrainMaze test potential treatments first in the avatar before going to the patient. The success in the medicine leads to an even greater success for BrainMaze as a tool for people to interact through a Brain-Computer Interface.

Title: *A Complex Journey*
        Book Two The Next Day
- Author: Randy McIntosh
- Publisher: TotalRecall Publications
- Paper Back: ISBN: 9781648831348
- eBook ISBN: 9781648831355
- Pages 200
- Publication Date: 2022

Brain-Computer Interfaces, Virtual Reality, Science and Espionage come together in a story about three scientists who work together to prevent a global climate disaster that appears to be caused by extra-terrestrial intruders.

www.ingramcontent.com/pod-product-compliance
Lightning Source LLC
Chambersburg PA
CBHW020636110726
47899CB00002B/785